A Christmas In Bath
(The Brides of Bath, Book 6)

The characters from the first five Brides of Bath books will be serving up some Christmas cheer, while Glee Blankenship sharpens Cupid's arrow.

Unbeknownst to scholarly Jonathan Blankenship, his sister-in-law Glee has decided this Christmas he needs a little push to make him see that his dear friend of four years, Miss Arbuckle, will make his perfect mate.

The Brides of Bath Series

"Bolen's writing has a certain elegance that lends itself to the era and creates the perfect atmosphere for her enchanting romances." — *RT Book Reviews*

Some of the praise for Cheryl Bolen's writing:

The Bride Wore Blue (Brides of Bath, Book 1)
"Cheryl Bolen returns to the Regency England she knows so well. . .If you love a steamy Regency with a fast pace, be sure to pick up *The Bride Wore Blue*." – *Happily Ever After*

Cheryl Bolen's writing draws you in to her fast-paced story. As you read, you grow to care about the characters and what happens to them. – *RT Book Reviews*, 4 STARS

With His Ring (Brides of Bath, Book 2)
"Cheryl Bolen does it again! There is laughter, and the interaction of the characters pulls you right into the book. I look forward to the next in this series." – *RT Book Reviews*

The Bride's Secret (Brides of Bath, Book 3)
(originally titled A Fallen Woman)
"*W*hat we all want from a love story...Don't miss it!"
– *In Print*

To Take This Lord (Brides of Bath, Book 4)
(originally titled An Improper Proposal)
"Bolen does a wonderful job building simmering sexual tension between her opinionated, outspoken heroine and deliciously tortured, conflicted hero." – *Booklist of the American Library Association*

With His Lady's Assistance (Regent Mysteries, Book 1)
Finalist for International Digital Award for Best Historical Novel of 2011.

"A delightful Regency romance with a clever and personable heroine matched with a humble, but intelligent hero. The mystery is nicely done, the romance is enchanting and the secondary characters are enjoyable." – *RT Book Reviews*

My Lord Wicked
Winner, International Digital Award for Best Historical Novel of 2011.

A Lady By Chance
"Cheryl Bolen has done it again with another sparkling Regency romance. . .Highly recommended." – *Happily Ever After*

A Duke Deceived
"A Duke Deceived is a gem. If you're a Georgette Heyer fan, if you enjoy the Regency period, if you like a genuinely sensuous love story, pick up this first novel by Cheryl Bolen." – *Happily Ever After*

One Golden Ring
"*One Golden Ring*...has got to be the most PERFECT Regency Romance I've read this year." – *Huntress Reviews*

Holt Medallion winner for Best Historical, 2006

The Counterfeit Countess
Daphne du Maurier award finalist for Best Historical Mystery

"This story is full of romance and suspense. . . No one can resist a novel written by Cheryl Bolen. Her writing talents charm all readers. Highly recommended reading! 5 stars!" – *Huntress Reviews*

"Bolen pens a sparkling tale, and readers will adore her feisty heroine, the arrogant, honorable Warwick and a wonderful cast of supporting characters." – *RT Book Reviews*

Protecting Britannia (Texas Heroines in Peril series)
"It's fun to watch the case unfold in this nonstop action adventure...Graham and Britannia's second chance at love adds dimension to the story." – 4 STARS *RT Book Reviews*

Cheryl Bolen's Books

Regency Historical Romance:

The Brides of Bath Series
  The Bride Wore Blue
  With His Ring
  The Bride's Secret
  To Take This Lord
  Love In The Library
  A Christmas in Bath

House of Haverstock Series
  Lady by Chance
  Duchess by Mistake
  Countess by Coincidence
  Ex-Spinster by Christmas

Brazen Brides Series
  Counterfeit Countess
  His Golden Ring
  Oh What A (Wedding) Night
  Miss Hastings' Excellent London Adventure
  A Birmingham Family Christmas

The Regent Mysteries Series
  With His Lady's Assistance
  A Most Discreet Inquiry
  The Theft Before Christmas
  An Egyptian Affair

A CHRISTMAS IN BATH

(The Brides of Bath, Book 6)

Cheryl Bolen

Copyright © 2014by Cheryl Bolen

A Christmas In Bath is a work of fiction. Names, characters, places, and incidents are the products of the author's imagination or are used fictitiously. Any resemblance to actual events, locales, or persons, living or dead, is entirely coincidental.

Chapter 1

When Miss Mary Arbuckle received the note from Glee Blankenship imploring her to come straight away to her house on Queen Square, Miss Arbuckle began to tremble. Had something happened to Jonathan Blankenship? It was not like Glee to order people about. Especially since Glee rather had her hands full with a new infant son and an entirely too precocious daughter not quite three years of age.

Miss Arbuckle wrapped herself in her faded red cape, put on her woolen gloves, twirled a muffler about her neck, and began the walk to Queen Square. Other young ladies subjected to the discomfort of walking in this extreme cold might have wished to command a luxurious coach and four to whisk them about this hilly watering city.

Unlike other girls, Miss Arbuckle's thoughts had never been occupied with wishing for things that were unobtainable. At a very early age she had come to accept that her widowed mother would never be possessed of wealth. She had also come to terms with the fact that she would never be a beauty. Her looking glass only too plainly confirmed that the most to which Miss Arbuckle could ever aspire was to be considered tolerable looking.

Because of her pragmatism, she had long accepted her fate as a spinster of extremely modest means. Such acceptance could have been sorely tried by the company she kept. Ever since she had attended Miss Worth's School for Young Ladies, her closest circle of friends had consisted of other young ladies of Quality who were in possession of beauty, wealth, and in many cases, rank.

Ten minutes of very fast walking brought her to the Blankenships' fine home. Inside, as she was divesting herself of her cape beneath a huge sparkling chandelier, the lovely Glee Blankenship came scurrying down the stairs to greet her.

Even though the two had been friends since they attended Miss Worth's School for Young Ladies together, Miss Arbuckle never failed to be struck over Glee's beauty. Perhaps it was because Glee was the antithesis of shy, drab, bookish Miss Arbuckle. Though Glee was considerably shorter than Miss Arbuckle, her vibrant personality was in perfect harmony with her fiery red hair, giving her a presence much larger than her stature would merit.

Only when Glee reached the gilt and marble entry corridor did Miss Arbuckle notice that she was carrying her babe. "I do thank you for coming, Miss Arbuckle! Please, let us go sit in the drawing room."

In the ivory drawing room, the butter-coloured silken draperies were open, providing the chamber with more light than other rooms, but it was still an excessively dreary day. It was, after all, December in Bath.

Glee sat opposite Miss Arbuckle, who had taken a seat upon one of a pair of silk brocade sofas that faced each other in front of the fire. Glee first addressed inarticulate noises to her little red-headed babe. Then, to Miss Arbuckle's astonishment, Glee lowered the bodice of her gown and lifted away that part of a woman's anatomy that provided sustenance. The babe began to greedily suckle.

Mary's cheeks turned scarlet. She had never before witnessed such a display! This was most shocking indeed. Miss Arbuckle was most determined to ignore what Glee was doing and concentrate on what she was saying.

It was, however, difficult not ponder the question of why Glee Blankenship had not procured a wet nurse. It was not as if Gregory Blankenship—Glee's husband—was not sinfully wealthy.

There was not the least trace of

embarrassment in Glee's voice when she spoke. "I wanted to tell you that Jonathan is coming to spend Christmas with us in Bath."

There was certainly nothing shattering in that remark. Why had Glee led Miss Arbuckle to believe the matter was so urgent? Then a thought, a truly petrifying thought, penetrated into Miss Arbuckle's brain. *He's bringing a wife.* Glee wanted to prepare Miss Arbuckle for the heart-breaking news.

Though the two women had never discussed Miss Arbuckle's feelings for Mr. Jonathan Blankenship, Glee had to know that her friend had loved him since the first day he had ever favored her with a comment.

Whenever he was in Bath, Jonathan Blankenship and Miss Arbuckle spent a great deal of time together, and the two of them shared many interests. He was the only young man who had ever danced with her at the Assembly Rooms, the only man who had ever brought her flowers, the only man who had ever honored her with his attentions.

Miss Arbuckle's eyes rounded. "Why should that matter to me?" Her disinterest, Glee had to know, was an act.

"I know very well, Mary Arbuckle, that you're in love with my brother-in-law. Can you deny it?"

Still fearing that Glee was going to notify her of Mr. Blankenship's nuptials, she shrugged. "I will own that I have a strong attachment to him, but there has never been any form of understanding between us."

"I know that very well, you goose! I have decided that you must give the man a little push so he'll realize you're the very woman to be his perfect wife."

Miss Arbuckle's sweating palms uncoiled, and she expelled the breath she was holding. He wasn't wed to another!

Then Glee's words sunk in. Miss Arbuckle had never allowed herself to give consideration to marrying dear Mr. Blankenship. "You forget that unlike you, I am not a beauty who can easily claim men's hearts. Nor am I possessed of fortune, and as a second son, Mr. Blankenship will surely be compelled to marry a woman who brings a comfortable dowry. I have resigned myself to being Mr. Blankenship's friend. Nothing more."

"Pooh! How long have you known him now?"

"Four years."

"And you are how old?"

Miss Arbuckle swallowed over her mortification. "The same as you. Three and twenty." An old maid, to be sure.

"I will not allow you to resign yourself to being a spinster." Glee deprived her babe of his nourishment, gently dabbed a cloth around his little mouth, and spoke some unintelligible nonsense to him.

All the while, Mary tried not to allow her gaze to drop below Glee's neck. "No one chooses to be a spinster. It just happens to be my fate."

"Pooh!" Glee began to nurse again, but Mary refused to let her eye lower.

"If Jonathan asked you to marry him, would you accept?" Glee asked.

Not without an alien fluttering in her heart, Miss Arbuckle nodded.

"Do you know, Miss Arbuckle, I am going to tell you something I have never told anyone before. Except for my sister-in-law Sally."

Miss Arbuckle quirked a brow.

"I employed every piece of cajolery possible in order to force myself into Blanks's heart."

Mary tossed her head back, laughing. "You cannot expect me to believe that. Everyone in Bath knows how insanely Mr. Blankenship loves you."

"I swear on my precious little son's life, Blanks never wanted to marry me."

Glee would never swear on her son's life were she not speaking the truth, the shocking, excessively-difficult-to-believe truth. "How can that be?"

"You know I loved him always?"

"Since you were twelve, if I recall correctly."

Glee nodded. "Even though he would lose

his fortune were he not wed by his twenty-fifth birthday, he turned down my offer to marry him so that he could secure his fortune. Next, I accused him of compromising my virtue so my brother would force him to wed me."

For the second time since she had taken a seat in the Blankenship drawing room, Miss Mary Arbuckle blushed scarlet. "It was a lie?"

Glee nodded sheepishly. "Then once we were married, I decided there was nothing I would not do to capture his heart."

"But as I said, it's easy for someone like you who's born beautiful to make men fall in love with you."

"It is my belief that Jonathan is already in love with you, but he just doesn't realize it. Now, Miss Arbuckle, we must plan our strategy."

Mary swallowed over the huge lump in her throat. "*Our* strategy?"

"Indeed. When I determined to capture Blanks's heart, I went about it in much the same way a general plans his battle strategy."

"Then you are far more clever than I."

"Jonathan would never agree with that. I declare, he has told me hundreds of times how uncommonly clever you are."

Miss Arbuckle warmed under such praise. "It would be false modesty for me to attempt to refute that for I realize that Mr.

Blankenship does credit me with thinking like an intelligent *man*. The pity of it is, he rather thinks of me as a man. To him, I am a very dear friend, like his friend Melvin Steffington. Nothing more."

"Then it is our job to make him see you with new eyes."

"New or old eyes, I am still plain."

"Being plain is not at all the same as being ugly. Because you are not ugly, it will be excessively easy to render you prettier. You must give me a free hand."

Miss Arbuckle shook her head. "It is difficult for one to appear pretty without pretty clothes, and I assure you, Mama's limited funds are stretched to the limit as it is."

"You are a good seamstress, are you not?"

She nodded. "But fabric comes very dearly."

"Sweet Sally gave me the dresses which she has been unable to get back into since the birth of her twins. She wanted me to find a good use for them. I got the brilliant idea that, since you are tallish like Sally, they will do very well for you—with modifications, of course. Your bosom is much larger than Sally's, which is non-existent."

How could Mrs. Blankenship speak of *bosom* without even lowering her voice? Once again, the flush stole into Miss Arbuckle's cheeks.

Miss Arbuckle would not recognize herself in fine ball gowns. She had never owned any. The very idea of wearing lovely clothes that had been made for a countess suffused Miss Arbuckle with a feeling of uncommon lightness. "I don't know. . ."

"I assure you, the gowns are lovely," Glee continued. "My brother selected them himself for her after he recovered from the fire, and now he is delighting himself by selecting new gowns for her."

"Are you certain Lady Sedgewick would not object?"

"Of course I am. Put your trust in me. When you go to the assemblies, it's essential you leave off the spectacles. Men are not attracted to them. Until they're in love with you. Then they love you just as you are."

"Whenever Jonathan Blankenship is in Bath, I do try to go without my spectacles."

"I know when the two of you are together sharing poems and treatises, you will have to wear them, but he's so obsessive over those pursuits I daresay he won't take a look at you."

That was true. "I don't believe he looks at me as a woman."

A wicked smile danced upon Glee's face. "I mean to change that."

"I don't know. . . It has occurred to me that

Mr. Blankenship is one of those men who is neither interested in women nor desirous of uniting himself to one."

"We will see, my dear Miss Arbuckle. We will see."

It was not in Mary Arbuckle's nature to be anything but compliant. "I shouldn't like to use trickery on dear Mr. Blankenship."

"I wouldn't call it trickery. It's simply a matter of assisting him to the place of his greatest happiness. What man would not wish to be there?"

"But how can you know where his happiness is?"

"Because he's my dear Blanks's brother! Trust me, Miss Arbuckle, I am a great student of human nature. I do know that he loves you. He first fell in love with your fine mind; now, he needs to be stunned by your appearance. "

Miss Arbuckle did hope she could put her faith in Glee's intuition. She had to credit Glee for the innate knowledge that Miss Arbuckle had fallen in love with Jonathan, though Miss Arbuckle had never admitted it to anyone. "I suppose your plan would only work were the gentleman willing."

"He will be willing."

Glee's little son had fallen to sleep. As Glee went to restore her clothing, Miss Arbuckle effected great interest in the fire blazing in the hearth.

"There is more!" Glee added.

Miss Arbuckle's stomach felt as if she were falling from a great height. "Dear God, tell me you have not told him of my feelings!"

Glee gently shook her head, then lowered her lashes to peer at her babe's sweet face.

Unaccountably, Miss Arbuckle felt a stab of envy. Not for Glee's beauty. Or for her wealth. But for the family she loved so dearly, the family that loved her just as devotedly.

"I have a plan to make Jonathan jealous," Glee said.

"There is nothing that would make him jealous because he is not in love with me."

"He is too. He just doesn't know it yet. It's our task to show him that of all the women in the wide world, you are the one who was created to be his mate."

Glee truly was possessed of a remarkable understanding of human nature for she had just perfectly described how Miss Arbuckle felt about Jonathan Blankenship. "One would have to be very adept at conjuring to accomplish such a feat."

"Conjuring has nothing to do with it. Because I *know* he loves you, I know that when he thinks another man wishes to steal your affections, he will do everything in his power to woo you."

Miss Arbuckle's mouth gaped open in

astonishment. "Another man? It appears my conjuring reference was justified."

"There *will* be another man. Leave that to me."

"I will own, you have far more experience than I in matters of love, my dear Mrs. Blankenship, but I cannot give credit to what you're saying."

"You admitted you would like to marry Jonathan. Now you must allow me to ensure that it happens." Glee rose. "Come up to my chamber so I can begin your physical transformation. He arrives this afternoon, and I mean for you to nearly steal his breath away."

* * *

Jonathan Blankenship simply could not spend another Christmas at Sutton Manor with his embittered mother. Neither he nor she had enjoyed Christmas since his father died more than four years previously.

One of the reasons he had come to his half-brother Gregory's place in Bath was to mend his family. Jonathan and his mother had a plan that Jonathan hoped to put forward in the next few days. Their family had been estranged for too long.

Gregory—known to his friends as Blanks—was so bitter toward Jonathan's mother that he almost never came to the family home since he had inherited it four years previously. It was really quite noble of him to allow Mama to continue at Sutton Manor when she had never shown affection for Gregory.

Now that Gregory had children, though, Mama was possessed of a tender affection for her grandchildren. She was forever sending them little presents, forever talking about them.

As Jonathan thought of his little niece, a smile crossed his face. Both he and his mother had selected presents for her, and he was excessively looking forward to sharing this Yule with his brother's family. As he thought of Gregory's new little son, he realized he would enjoy the next Christmas even more because then the lad would be fun to play with.

At seven and twenty years of age, Jonathan Blankenship had accepted that he would never marry, never sire children. He would settle for being an uncle.

As he stood on the step to Gregory and Glee's house on Queen Square, he heard little Joy's sweet voice. He let himself in—as Glee had insisted he do. "You must always consider our home your home," she had said any number of times.

"Uncle Jona-fin," Joy squealed, running to him on her toddler legs, her arms opened wide.

He lifted her high in the air, then kissed her sweet little golden curls.

"Did you bwing me a pwesent?"

"Now why should I bring you a present?"

"Because you always do."

"I did, but this present is tied with a bow and cannot be opened until Christmas."

"Can I see it?"

"Later, love."

"Will you give me a piggy-back ride?"

He proceeded to hike her upon his shoulders, careful not to lose his grip of her tiny hands, and began to walk from the morning room to the drawing room to the dinner room, then back to the porter's hall.

There, Joy's exasperated nurse stood, giving the child a mock glare. "I've been looking all over for ye! It is time to take yer nap, pet."

Joy's lower lip protruded. "I don't want to!"

"If you go along with Nurse like a good little girl," Jonathan said, "I shall give you a sweet when you awaken." He set her down, and she walked obligingly to her nurse.

After seeing if any post had come for him—and finding that none had—Jonathan began to mount the stairs to the library. On the stairs a young woman was coming down. He gave her a curt nod, said "Good day," and continued on.

"Mr. Blankenship!"

By God, he recognized that voice! It sounded like Miss Arbuckle, though the woman he had just passed bore no resemblance to her. He stopped dead in his stride and pivoted toward the lady, whose progress had also been halted.

They stood there staring at one another. He was powerless to keep his lazy gaze from moving to the Grecian style of her dark, fetching hair, along her sweet face with its eyes as black as currants, then to her. . . bosom. My God, Miss Arbuckle was possessed of a bosom! And a very womanly bosom at that. For some confounded reason, he could barely catch his breath, and against all his control, this . . . this attractive Miss Arbuckle had a profound effect upon him. *Below the waist.*

He was not at all pleased. "What the devil's happened to you?"

"Glee has taken it into her mind that I must take more pains with my appearance."

"There was nothing wrong with your appearance before," he snapped, his mouth settling into a grim line.

"But, you must own, I have failed to attract a husband."

Glee came rushing down the stairs. "But now that Miss Arbuckle is having her hair styled to go along with her stunning new dresses, she has any number of suitors." Glee came to hug him. "Good day, dear Jonathan. We are so thrilled you've come for Christmas. Your presence will make it our happiest yet."

He nodded curtly to Glee, then turned back to Miss Arbuckle. "How can you see without your spectacles?"

The lady shrugged. And he noticed her shoulders were exposed. Creamy, silken shoulders. No wonder she had suitors knocking down her door! He did not like this transformation that had come over his old friend. Why could she not be content with life the way it was?

"I mostly need them to read," she answered.

"Speaking of reading, I was on my way to the library to peruse the new edition of the *Edinburgh Review.* Have you seen it?" He knew the lady's widowed mother was unable to pay for subscriptions to the publications her scholarly daughter enjoyed reading. Miss Arbuckle was the only person he had ever known whose reading interests so closely mirrored his own. He was even closer to her than he was to Melvin Steffington, whose interests channeled into classicism, while he and Miss Arbuckle were keenly interested in political thought.

"No, I haven't had the opportunity," she said.

"Why do you not join me in the library?" He

felt awkward asking such a . . . a voluptuous woman to come sit beside him. Oddly, he had a compulsion to peer at the tops of her generous breasts. Why had he never before noticed that Miss Arbuckle was. . . womanly? Damn those suitors!

A knock upon the entry door distracted him, and he turned to see who was there. The butler took a small bouquet, nodded, and said, "I shall see that Miss Arbuckle gets these."

Jonathan glared as Hampton moved toward Miss Arbuckle and presented her with the nosegay.

Her dark brows rose in query. "Are you certain these are for me?"

"Indeed," the butler said.

She took them, then found a piece of folded-up paper pinned to them. After unfolding it, she read the brief note. He tried his demdest to see the signature of the man who sent the flowers, but she quickly refolded the note, tucked it into a pocket, and then shoved her nose in to the white blooms. "Are they not lovely, Mr. Blankenship?"

"Daresay the fellow's got a hot house. How else could blooms like that be procured in December?" If the fellow had a hot house, that could mean he was possessed of a fine house. And wealth too, most probably. A wealthy man would not mind that Miss

Arbuckle had no dowry.

Jonathan found himself regretting that he'd left Bath several weeks earlier. Had he known Miss Arbuckle was going to go about displaying her . . . her fleshy bits and her milky shoulders, he would have stayed here and put his foot down! She obviously needed a steadying presence such as himself. Certainly not Glee!

Was Miss Arbuckle not going to tell him who her admirer was? He did not like this at all. He and Miss Arbuckle never kept secrets from one another. When Jeremy Bentham had quietly come to Bath for the waters, she was one of the few who had learned of the great philosopher's secret presence in Bath. Though she had been told to tell no one, she found it impossible to conceal Mr. Bentham's presence from him, a huge admirer of Bentham's *for the greater good* political teachings.

She shared many other things with him. She was the first to suspect that Glee was increasing with their son, and she shared that too with him. And of all their mutual acquaintances, he was the only one who knew what a fine poet she was. For she shared her impressive works only with him.

And now she was being courted. He swallowed. Would he lose her friendship?

The very notion put him in a foul temper.

"I do hate to disappoint you," Glee said to him, "but Miss Arbuckle must rush home to prepare for the Assembly Rooms tonight."

He glared at Glee, glared at Miss Arbuckle. "Then I shall see you—and your suitors—there." His fists clenched, he pounded up the stairs.

Chapter 2

Though it was against her nature to show anger, Miss Arbuckle could not conceal her displeasure with Glee Blankenship. Miss Arbuckle had ever so much wanted to go into the library with Mr. Blankenship.

Once he had slammed the library door, she directed a shocked gaze at Glee. "You've gotten me in a fine fix! What shall I do at the Assembly Rooms tonight? Mr. Blankenship will be expecting me to have admirers, and you know I have none."

Glee gave a smug smile. "I am not above inventing admirers for you. Was that not clever of me to have those flowers sent to you?"

Miss Arbuckle frowned. "At first I was foolish enough to believe I actually had an admirer, then I realized how cunning you can be. I am mortified, I assure you, by all this."

Glee continued to descend the stairs. "My carriage should be here now. Come, Miss Arbuckle, allow me to take you home. It's beastly weather for you to be walking in."

After they both wrapped themselves in warm garb, they got into the fine Blankenship coach, sitting opposite each other. "Did you notice how Jonathan could not remove his eyes from your very fine breasts?"

There went the scarlet—this time colouring Miss Arbuckle's entire face. "I have never been so embarrassed."

Glee turned a shocked gaze upon her. "You cannot be serious! Do you not realize it is a very good thing when a man becomes aware of a woman's sexuality?"

Oh, dear. No one had ever uttered the word *sexuality* in front of Miss Mary Arbuckle before. And to think it was being used in connection with her! She was truly mortified. "I shall die if Mr. Blankenship thinks me fast."

Glee began to giggle. "You and I must be vastly different. I wanted Blanks to think me fast so he would want to bed me—then fall in love with me. Men have much more prominent sexual desires than women, you know. They often fall in love with women who satisfy their primal needs."

Miss Arbuckle clapped her hands over her ears. "I cannot listen to such talk." Truth be told, she did not believe Jonathan Blankenship like other men. A man possessed of so fine a mind would not be interested in carnal pleasures. Never had a single breath been uttered that linked him to brothels or doxies or other such pursuits many other young men were attracted to.

Before today, he had never shown the slightest sign that he thought of her as anything other than a dear friend. Exactly as he felt toward Dr. Melvin Steffington.

Yet today, when his simmering gaze had so slowly raked over her breasts, she felt as if she had stood there completely naked. He had never looked at her in such a way before.

"I hope you do not mind," said Glee, "if we go by Blanks's solicitor's place of business."

"I am just happy for a warm, dry ride."

"I don't know about it actually being warm. I wish I'd brought my muff."

Miss Arbuckle thought of Glee's ermine muff. But without envy. She had long ago schooled herself not to want for that which she could not have. She stuffed her gloved hands into the quilted silken muff she had made for herself with scraps given her by Glee's sister, Felicity.

"I am sure I will be warm enough when you go in to see the solicitor."

"Oh, I'm not going to actually see the solicitor. I just want to see that the little urchin there is warm enough. And his mother, too. I told you about her sad condition before, did I not?"

"The woman whose life is governed by gin?"

A look of incredible sadness passed over Glee's face. "For four years now we've been trying to bring Mrs. A. into service for us. Then I would know her little Archie is being properly cared for."

"But she knows she is unable to give up her wicked liquid sustenance?"

Glee nodded solemnly. "At the time we married, Blanks swore that she had one foot already in the grave, but she's still alive—though I declare you've never seen anyone who's more thin than she is."

Moments later, Miss Arbuckle was able to verify the veracity of Glee's statement when the carriage pulled up in front of the establishment where Mrs. A. cleaned. When Mrs. A. was lucid enough to know where she was supposed to be.

Miss Arbuckle sickened as she watched the frail young woman come ambling down the front steps, her young son attempting to hold her up. Miss Arbuckle had never seen a skinnier woman. Her arms—even though covered by many layers of tattered clothing—were barely bigger around than a billiards stick, and her face so thin it more closely resembled a skeleton than a woman in her twenties. Her hair was filthy, like the rest of her, and it was difficult to speculate what colour it had once been. Perhaps a dark blonde? Upon her feet were a man's boots that were not only much too large for her, but they were also punctured by holes.

So young to die, Miss Arbuckle thought of the young mother.

"I am pleased to see Archie wearing the warm boots and coat I bought for him, but his mother must have sold the woolen cape I got her."

Miss Arbuckle could not bear to look at the unfortunate woman. She turned back to Glee and spoke somberly. "Sold it to buy gin, no doubt. Will you get her another?"

"I can't have her freeze to death."

The coach continued on. "I don't need to stop," Glee said. "I was worried about Archie, but I'm satisfied his mother didn't sell his warm coat."

"You surely did not expect a mother to deprive her child!"

Glee answered with a morose nod. "It wouldn't be the first time. She sold his coat last winter. I wanted so gravely to bring the lad to live with us, but he's . . ." She sadly shook her head. "He's very attached to her. It's more like she's his child—rather than the other way around."

Seeing the plight of little Archie and his mother reinforced Mary's gratitude that she had been born to a middle-class family, reinforced her contentment with her meager lot in life.

She wiped the fogginess from the window and peered out as the coach rattled along in front of Bath Cathedral.

"You will never guess who I saw in Bath yesterday," Glee exclaimed. "Well not to where I'd speak to him—which I wouldn't—but from a distance."

"I know of no one whom you excessively dislike."

"Yes, you do, but she will be in prison for a very long while. In fact, she's fortunate she wasn't hanged."

Miss Arbuckle's eyes widened. "You must have seen that evil Miss Johnson's father, but did you not know she died in prison? In childbed."

"She was married?"

"No. It is my understanding that her wickedness extended to other forms of loose conduct."

"Did Mr. Johnson get the babe?"

"The babe died too."

"I know I shall sound wicked, but I am not sorry Betsy Johnson is dead. Not after all the pain and financial loss she caused my brother." A look of disgust flashed across Glee's face. "I thought her father had left England after the shame of his daughter's trial and conviction."

"I thought so too." Miss Arbuckle found herself looking along the streets for signs of Mr. Johnson. "I always felt rather sorry for him. It wasn't his fault his only child was so wicked."

"I cannot feel sorry for him after the way he tried to bribe the jury. As a parent, I understand wanting to help your child, but a parent also has the responsibility to allow children to be punished when they've done bad things."

"True."

"Now, for something less melancholy. . . " Glee began. "I am certain my plan is working. Could you not hear the angry inflection in Jonathan's voice when he was informed of your suitors? I vow, he was not pleased to see how pretty you look for he doesn't want other men to notice you."

"The only reason other men would notice me is because you've got me spilling out of Lady Sedgewick's dresses!"

"You mustn't say that."

"But my . . . " (Miss Arbuckle simply could not refer to that part of her anatomy), "I *am* spilling out."

"What I meant is that you must not call your gown Sally's. All of them are now yours."

Miss Arbuckle was still upset about going to the Assembly Rooms that night. "I cannot go tonight."

"Why do you say that?"

"Because I have no men in a queue to dance with me."

"I shall take care of that."

"Oh, dear."

A moment later, Miss Arbuckle was being deposited at her modest home. "Since it's so cold," Glee told her, "we will call for you tonight."

"I cannot go."

"Do not fret about what to wear. As we speak, my maid is finishing the adjustments to the gown you'll wear tonight. I'll send it along."

"Mr. Blankenship will see that I am still a wallflower."

"Oh, no, he won't. I have a plan."

* * *

He disliked going to the Assembly Rooms, but when in Bath it was a necessary evil. Only at the Assembly Rooms was he assured of meeting with his friends. Unlike his popular brother, though, Jonathan only had two friends in Bath: Miss Arbuckle and Melvin. The lady was, in fact, the only female friend he had ever had.

Sadly, his friendship with Melvin had changed considerably since Melvin had married this past year. Jonathan was still scratching his head over Melvin's marriage. His friend—unlike Melvin's twin, Sir Elvin, and Sir Elvin's friend, Appleton—had never been in the petticoat line. Not ever.

It was still a complete mystery to Jonathan how that Mrs. Bexley had captured his friend's heart—which is certainly what she had done. The transformation that had come over Melvin was elliptical. He had gone from total disinterest in women to being besotted over the lady.

Jonathan could not understand what there was about the former Mrs. Bexley to have so thoroughly ensnared Melvin. She was not nearly as intelligent nor as well read as Miss Arbuckle. He must own that she would be considered pretty, but previously Melvin had never taken notice of such, much less succumbed to something as fleeting as beauty.

Jonathan could not understand how his friend could prefer to be with his new wife and not come to Blankenship House for one of their lively discussions on the ancient philosophers. One would think the man would get tired of so unvarying a relationship. Women—except for Miss Arbuckle—were so deadly dull.

Now Jonathan had but one friend who remained unencumbered by marriage, and it was looking as if that too would soon be snatched away from him. How could Miss Arbuckle not be content to continue on with her widowed mother? It was so unlike her to want to become someone's wife.

He frowned. What would he do if she should marry? He did not think he could come to Bath again, for being with her was one of the largest enticements to coming to this city. Were she to marry and be put into her husband's pocket, Jonathan would be robbed of his dearest friend.

As the Blankenship coach pulled up in front of Miss Arbuckle's house that night, he pictured her as she had looked that afternoon. He most certainly hoped she did not continue displaying herself in such a revealing manner! No wonder the men were likely making cakes of themselves over her!

In the coach she sat beside him, opposite his brother and Glee. He was unable to determine what she wore, for a rather thick cape enveloped her. She had once again left off her spectacles, and her hair looked as it had that afternoon. Did not suit her at all. Miss Arbuckle's neat little dark brown bun at the nape of her neck was as much a part of her as her keen intelligence. Why did she have to go and try to fancy herself up? These new, spiraling tresses—like her new manner of dress—were entirely too provocative.

"Do you not think Miss Arbuckle's hair becoming?" Glee asked him.

He grunted. "It's so different from what I'm accustomed to."

"You'll get used to it," Glee said.

He turned to Miss Arbuckle. "Surely you're not going to persist in fancying yourself up."

"Your sister-in-law says I must," Miss Arbuckle answered in her meek little voice.

"Don't know why you think you have to be married. What will your mother do without you?"

"I hope I will be able to continue living in Bath—after I am wed."

Hearing her discuss her nuptials oddly made his stomach drop. He would not like it at all if she were to marry. And what man could be worthy of someone with all her attributes? Melvin was the only one he knew, and he was already married!

Then it struck him that she might already have someone. One man upon whom she had bestowed her affections. And his stomach felt as if he had eaten something rotten.

When they reached the Assembly Rooms, he assisted in removing her woolen cape. When he saw that she wore an elegant ivory gown with a very, very low-cut neckline, his stomach once again plummeted.

Since the orchestra was beginning a new set, he quickly claimed her. "Will you honor me by standing up with me, Miss Arbuckle?"

She offered him a gentle nod and laced her arm with his as they strode onto the dance floor. As they stood facing one another on the longway, he found he could not remove his eyes from her. Though he did not like this change that had come over her one whit, he believed other men would be attracted to her.

Why had he never before noticed how smooth and creamy her skin was? His gaze moved to the ladies on either side of her, both of whom wore dresses which did little to hide their breasts, and he thought neither of them was in possession of skin as lovely as Miss Arbuckle's. And certainly none of them had eyes nearly as fine as hers. A pity she had not worn her spectacles. Other men would be sure to want to claim someone as fetching as she looked.

He had never failed to dance with her when he attended the Assembly Rooms these past four years, so why was it now that when their hands touched, he experienced an unfamiliar jolt to his insides?

After the dance, he offered to procure tea for her. When he returned to the crowded, noisy ballroom mere minutes later, she was dancing with Appleton. Not just a country dance like she had just favored him with, but she and Appleton were waltzing!

Never before had Appleton danced with Miss Arbuckle. He had always preferred women who were. . . less respectable.

Had it been any other man—as in, married man—Jonathan would not have objected in the least, but Appleton was a notorious rake. Look at the way his hand tried to cradle her to him! And Jonathan was certain Appleton was staring at Miss Arbuckle's breasts.

He was seized with a strong desire to send his fist crashing into Appleton's lecherous face. As he stood there seething with anger toward his brother's old friend, it suddenly became clear to Jonathan that he would have to serve as protector to poor Miss Arbuckle. What did a shy bluestocking like she know of rakes like Appleton? She might only see that the fellow was most comfortably fixed, and it was no secret that Miss Arbuckle was not at all well fixed.

Why, she might look at Appleton as a prize. Nothing could be further from the truth! Truth be told, Appleton was a profligate of the first order. Unless things had dramatically changed since Jonathan had last been in Bath, Appleton kept one Mrs. Vale in a *love* nest on Water Street.

And the man's interests were not in the least compatible with Miss Arbuckle's, either. His knowledge was so lacking, he would think Thomas Paine a sickly man named Thomas. Appleton cared only for gaming, race meetings, and lascivious ladies of the night.

It fairly sickened Jonathan to contemplate an alliance between sweet Miss Arbuckle and that. . . that rake. A pity she no longer dressed in the modest clothing he was accustomed to seeing her wearing. Yes, there was nothing for it but for Jonathan to watch out for her best interests. After all, she had neither father nor brother.

When Appleton walked her back to Jonathan at the end of the set, Jonathan snapped at her. "Your tea's cold."

She took it. "Thank you, Mr. Blankenship, I rather like cold tea."

He nodded, then directed his attention at Appleton. "Where is your partner in revelry tonight?"

Appleton looked down his nose at Jonathan (who, regrettably, was considerably shorter than Appleton). "To whom could you be referring?"

"Sir Elvin." Even though Jonathan had been close friends with Sir Elvin's twin these many years, it still seemed incredible to him that the two men were from the same womb for serious-minded Melvin was the antithesis of his brother.

"He said he'd be here."

"And his brother?" Jonathan inquired.

Appleton's eye moved to the door. "Here comes Melvin. Catherine Steffington looks lovely tonight, even though her time draws near. I never thought old Melvin had so good an eye for beautiful women." Then his gaze dropped to Miss Arbuckle's bodice. "Speaking of which, does not Miss Arbuckle look fetching tonight?"

Jonathan very nearly stormed to the cloak

room in order to procure Miss Arbuckle's cloak to cover her from Appleton's greedy gawk. He stepped right in front of Appleton in order to block the lecher's view of Miss Arbuckle's. . .gulp, *breasts*. "I liked her the way she used to look!" Jonathan snapped.

Appleton chuckled, then stuck his head over Jonathan's shoulder and peered at the lady. "I do thank you, Miss Arbuckle, for standing up with me."

"The honor was mine, Mr. Appleton," she said.

"I say, Miss Arbuckle," Jonathan said after Appleton left them, "I would be gratified if you would stand up with me again."

He had not noticed that his sister-in-law had strolled up to them. "Now see here, Jonathan, you cannot monopolize Miss Arbuckle. You must give the other men the opportunity to dance with her."

Why was it that Glee was becoming a thorn in his side? Whenever he would be about to have dear Miss Arbuckle to himself, Glee would interfere.

Miss Arbuckle's gaze shifted from him to Glee. She was prevented from answering when Melvin and his bride joined them. "I say, Blankenship," Melvin said to Jonathan, "it's devilishly good to see you back in Bath. Pray, do me the goodness of joining me in the Octagon so I can discuss your latest essay with you."

Jonathan tossed a morose look at Miss Arbuckle, then nodded to his friend. What the devil was coming over him? He had always excessively enjoyed discussing his essays with Melvin Steffington, but now he found himself wishing to stay by Miss Arbuckle's side to keep those profligates from sullying her sweetness.

* * *

For the first time in her life, to Miss Arbuckle's complete astonishment, she was not a wallflower. In the past, only the two Blankenship brothers had spared her from sitting out every single dance. And, when Glee's brother was in town, Lord Sedgewick could be depended upon to favor her with a dance. She suspected Glee's gallant husband was happy indeed that he would not have to stand up with her this night.

When the final waltz of the night was struck up, and Jonathan Blankenship sought her for his partner, she came to realize she had never enjoyed an assembly more. She felt rather like a princess because of the attentions she had drawn.

What a pity it was that the only man whose opinion she courted did not think her hair becoming.

She knew she would not be able to persist with her vastly improved appearance. It was not as if she could have Glee's maid dress her hair every day, and she could no more arrange her own hair with such artistry than she could read a book without her spectacles. She had to own that despite feeling like a princess, she had been far more comfortable in her familiar old clothes that did not make her feel as if she were unclothed.

"It seems you were a great success tonight," Mr. Blankenship said to her, "though I daresay none of your partners were up to snuff."

"What do you mean up to snuff? I thought they were all delightful." Particularly her present partner.

"I mean marriageable."

"Oh. I did not realize. Perhaps I shall need your counsel." Glee had suggested she say that to him.

"Indeed you do. Since you have neither father nor brother, I think it's best you allow me guide you. After all, I am older than you, and I've been more in the world than have you, my dear Miss Arbuckle."

"You would do that for me?"

"Of course. You are, after all, one of my dearest friends."

She sighed. "That is the worst thing about becoming someone's wife. I shan't be able to continue our friendship, Mr. Blankenship, and I do value it excessively." Glee had encouraged her to say that too.

He squeezed at her waist, where his hand rested, and her heartbeat drummed madly. He had never done that a single time in the last four years. "I don't mind telling you, I shouldn't like to lose your friendship either."

"Perhaps my husband won't mind. It's not as if you think of me as a man thinks of a woman." That, too, had been Glee's suggestion.

"I beg that you give me credit for knowing the difference between a man and a woman."

"I don't mean to imply that you don't."

"I would hope you don't confuse me with any of your female friends."

She paused. "No, I don't believe I have ever taken you for one of my female friends."

In the carriage ride home after the assembly, he said, "What a difference three months can make. The last time I was in Bath the weather easily permitted us to walk to and from the assemblies, and now it's so beastly cold I am happy for my brother's carriage."

Then he directed his attention at Glee. "Would you be adverse to me borrowing the coach tomorrow to take Miss Arbuckle for a spin through Sydney Gardens?"

"I have always told you that when you're in Bath you are to treat our house and our carriage as if they're yours, but I daresay

Miss Arbuckle's likely made plans for tomorrow. You must have noticed how sought after she's become."

She knew Glee would not approve, but Miss Arbuckle was far too eager to be with Mr. Blankenship. "Actually, I don't have plans. I should love to go for a drive with you tomorrow."

Chapter 3

The following morning Glee, along with her sister Felicity, and Melvin Steffington's bride, the former Catherine Bexley, paid a morning call upon Mary Arbuckle. Other young ladies (well, perhaps not so young) might have been embarrassed to have the daughters of a viscount calling at their modest homes, but because of Miss Arbuckle's long association with the sisters, she knew they judged friends not on possessions but on amiability.

They had often surprised her with a visit—to Mrs. Arbuckle's delight. Though rarely in Society, Mary's mother was enough of an eager follower of Society to be humbled and pleased over such a connection to the *nobility*.

Mary greeted the visitors in the small drawing room at the front of their skinny little house. The visitors sat one after another on a faded chintz sofa, and Mary faced them in an arm chair a bit closer to the fire.

"As much as I adore your mother," Glee began, "I wanted a private word with you." Her gaze flicked to Felicity and Catherine. "They don't count. They know everything."

The sisters were Mary's lifelong friends, but

she was not as well acquainted with Catherine, who was a bit older and closer to Felicity. How mortified Miss Arbuckle was to think Catherine knew she fancied herself in love with Jonathan Blankenship! The heat suffusing her cheeks, Miss Arbuckle's gaze darted straight to Catherine. "Everything?"

Catherine nodded meekly. "Your affection for Jonathan Blankenship very much reminds me of how I felt about Airy—before he fell in love with me." *Airy* was Catherine's own name for Melvin, owing to her calling her scholar husband *Aristotle.*

Miss Arbuckle's embarrassment faded, and her attention perked. Jonathan Blankenship *was* very much like Melvin Steffington, in that neither of them had been possessed of a womanizing bent—unlike the men's friends— all of whom had set up women as mistresses at one time or another. Well, all except for Felicity's husband, who never wanted any woman save Felicity. Unlike the scholarly pursuits that absorbed Jonathan's and Melvin's interests, though, Thomas Moreland directed his attentions to the making of a fortune—a talent for which he was most adept.

Before Miss Arbuckle could comment, Glee continued on. "That's why I have brought my dear Mrs. Steffington here today. We must find out what means she used to encourage a declaration from Melvin."

Were any other woman to refer to men by their Christian names, they would meet with censure. But not Glee Blankenship. Her lively personality won approval even from Society's strictest critics.

Catherine's shoulders shrugged. "I don't think I was aware of doing anything in particular. I do believe I was the first to fall in love, but I never dreamed I would be able to capture his heart. You know how that is, Miss Arbuckle, with serious-minded men like Jonathan and Airy."

"Indeed I do. It's my belief that Jonathan Blankenship has never been interested in those of the female gender—in the same way most other young men are."

"Exactly what I thought about Airy! And later I learned I was right. I was his first."

All this talk of love and young men's *other* interests sent Miss Arbuckle's thoughts off in a direction in which they had seldom travelled. She found herself wondering if Catherine meant she was the first woman Melvin (Airy) had ever loved, or was she referring to being the first woman he had ever . . . gulp, bedded.

"So, did you try to make him jealous?" Miss Arbuckle asked.

Catherine did not reply for a moment, then Mary understood why. She was trying not to offend the plain spinster. For Catherine, with her flaxen hair and lovely face and figure, already had other suitors when she began her association with Melvin. Unlike Mary, who had never had a single suitor.

Catherine finally shook her head. "Our relationship began upon a shared goal. I begged him to use his scholarly skills to help find the nearly priceless Chaucer that was stolen from me. That shared goal forced us to spend a great deal of time together." The lady sighed. "Soon I was deeply in love him."

Felicity's brows plunged. "Can you perhaps pinpoint a certain occurrence that pushed him from friend to lover?"

Catherine thought on this for a moment. "I suppose it was the kiss."

"You kissed him?" a shocked Miss Arbuckle asked.

A slow smile curled on Catherine's contented face. "He kissed me, actually. Then, he apologized profusely—when all I really wanted was more kisses."

Miss Arbuckle sighed. If only she were pretty like Catherine Steffington. "I have been alone with Mr. Blankenship any number of times these past four years, and he's never had the urge to kiss me. I don't believe men like Jonathan Blankenship are interested in kissing."

Ten months ago Miss Arbuckle would have

said the same thing about Melvin Steffington.

Felicity's amused gaze whisked to her sister, and the two women burst out laughing.

"Pray, what is so funny?" Miss Arbuckle asked.

Felicity could not wipe the smile from her face. "The man has not been created who is disinterested in kissing."

Glee nodded her assent.

Miss Arbuckle's gaze swept to Catherine, who also nodded. "It's true, Miss Arbuckle, even for men like my Airy and your Jonathan."

Your Jonathan. Oh, how Miss Arbuckle liked the sound of that! (Though the idea of Melvin Steffington kissing was most vexing.) Miss Arbuckle eyed Catherine's belly and saw the proof of their ardor in the babe she was carrying.

Glee put her hands to her hips and directed a mock glare at Mary. "You somewhat foiled my plan last night when you readily agreed to allow Jonathan to take you to the park this afternoon."

"But it's been nearly four months since I last saw him," Mary defended. "I have been saving up so many things I've been wanting to talk to him about. Why, he's had two different essays—very fine ones—published over the past two months. I'm ever so anxious to discuss these with him."

"I think she's right, Glee," Catherine said. "Allow her to be alone with him. Perhaps he shall be overcome with the desire to steal a kiss from her, and we know what that can lead to."

"Marriage!" Felicity's blue eyes brightened.

Glee continued to pout. "My plan was to throw up encumbrances to their being together so that when they finally did. . ." Her face softened, and she sighed. "He would barely be able to control his burgeoning desire for her!"

The three married ladies all giggled.

Miss Arbuckle turned crimson.

"Do you know," Glee continued, "I cajoled Appleton to dance attendance upon Miss Arbuckle last night—which he did to please me—but at the end of the night he confided in me that he thought she was *bang up to scratch.*"

"After you left the assembly rooms," Catherine added, "Mr. Appleton told Melvin he just might be calling upon Miss Arbuckle."

"How delightful!" Glee's eyes sparked with mirth.

But Mary did not want Appleton calling upon her. She wanted only Mr. Blankenship.

"By the way, Miss Arbuckle," Glee said, "my maid will be here shortly. I'm sending her along to assist with your hair so you'll dazzle my brother-in-law this afternoon."

* * *

What the devil was the matter with him, Jonathan wondered as he rode in his brother's coach to Miss Arbuckle's house. He'd had the opportunity to bring up the subject of Mama paying a Christmas visit at Gregory's, but his courage had failed him.

There was less than a week remaining before Christmas, and if Gregory and Glee would consent to have Mama, she would need to leave Sutton Manor soon. Especially since the roads were so bloody icy.

Perhaps he should approach Glee first. The difficulty there was that Glee—normally possessed of a most obliging nature—got her hackles all bristly whenever Mama was mentioned. It was times like that Glee seemed less a wife and more a protective mother. More than once she had told Jonathan that she thought his mother's coolness toward Gregory was intolerable.

Now that Jonathan was a grown man, he agreed. He bitterly regretted that he had allowed his mother to show her preference for him—her own son—over his popular elder brother, whom everyone else wildly preferred.

When the coach stopped in front of Miss Arbuckle's house, Jonathan wondered what she would be wearing today. Surely she would not persist in exposing her. . . her delicate skin to such harsh winter elements. It was so beastly cold today that a light snow was falling.

Theirs would likely be the only coach in the gardens today. After all, no flowers were in bloom. The trees had shed their green. As he thought about it, he realized that when he had requested she go to Sydney Gardens with him, he had been recalling his last visit to Bath. Then, the weather was perfection, permitting him and Miss Arbuckle to walk there.

That day the two of them had spent at Sydney Gardens had stayed vivid in his memories these months of their separation. He'd never had a friend to whom he could speak so freely of all that he read, all his beliefs and desires. In his limited experience with the opposite gender, he believed women the inferior sex, as far as intelligence.

But Miss Arbuckle refuted that belief. In every way, save her unfamiliarity with Greek and Latin, she was his intellectual equal.

She most certainly was not the sort of woman who went about making herself appear desirable. Desirable in the way Appleton found women desirable!

Good lord, what will I do if she gets herself married? He would lose the best friend he ever had. Why could she not continue wearing her high-necked dresses and spectacles? It was as if she were misrepresenting herself to a future husband!

His knowledge of Miss Arbuckle assured him that she would never intentionally misrepresent herself. This had to be Glee's doing!

He braved the cold, hissing winds to rap upon the Arbuckle's peeling front door. Normally, he was admitted by a thin, stern housekeeper, but today Miss Arbuckle herself opened the door. "I didn't want you having to stand in the cold," she said, smiling broadly upon him.

His gaze went first to the cluster of curls artfully framing her face—a face without spectacles! Then his gaze dropped to that creamy expanse of skin. "I cannot be responsible if you should take your death of cold in that dress."

"I would never hold you responsible, Mr. Blankenship." She gathered up a woolen spencer and handed it to him. "Will you assist me, please?"

He took the little piece of frippery that would cover her shoulders, though it would not provide much warmth. As he lay it upon those smooth ivory shoulders, his heartbeat raced. "There you go."

She slowly turned and favored him with a smile, then reached down and lifted her faded red cloak. "And this, too, please."

Now here was a piece of her clothing he recognized. And with great fondness, too. He placed it upon her shoulders, tied it below her chin, and found that his heartbeat was racing again. A sense of well-being filled him as he became aware of the subtle smell of roses. Where in the devil did roses come from in the dead of winter?

Then, to his dismay, his gaze alighted on not one but two bouquets (neither of which happened to be roses) upon the sideboard. Good lord, did she have *two* suitors?

"Just as soon as I put on my gloves, I shall be ready to go," said she.

Once she was bundled up for warmth—to his great satisfaction—he proffered his arm and led her to the coach. He was not accustomed to offering Miss Arbuckle his arm. It was the demmed hair and revealing clothing that made him much too aware of her gender. Why could she not be content to be his good friend? Why must she persist in acting like a woman? Miss Arbuckle never before acted like other members of her sex.

The difference between her and other women was what accounted for his great friendship with her.

In the coach, she sat opposite him—as she normally did when it was just the two of them, which only occurred during the coldest months of the year. He would not allow the coachman to start until Jonathan was assured that he had covered Miss Arbuckle in the rug's warmth. "Warm enough?" he asked.

"Yes, thank you."

Only then did they proceed.

"I apologize that it's not the kind of day one visits Sydney Gardens." Was it the mention of gardens that made him smell roses again?

"You mustn't apologize. It's not your fault it's so cold."

He gave a little laugh. "I suppose I was merely eager for an opportunity to be alone with you. I have missed our discussions whilst I've been at Sutton Manor."

"I have too. In fact, I've been ever so anxious to discuss with you that very fine essay you wrote against slavery."

He shrugged. "I daresay there's little need to keep lambasting such a brutal practice—at least here in England."

"It is our good fortune that so many of our countrymen are enlightened in their opposition to it."

"I did receive a great many positive comments about the anti-slavery essay." He drew his breath. "It was rather the opposite with my essay about labor unification."

She nodded thoughtfully. "Allow me to speculate. I daresay the big landowners were up in arms."

He had known she would instantly grasp

the situation. "You have the right of it. They claim if their laborers were paid a decent wage they would go bankrupt, have to sell off all their land, and then where would the country be when there was no work to be had?"

"Then your next essay needs to explain all the positives that can arise from a better paid citizenry."

"Exactly what I was thinking! In fact, I've already begun it. Would you do me the goodness of reading it to see if you think I'm approaching the subject in the right way?" There was no one whose opinion he valued more.

"I would be honored to."

His gaze moved to the heap of papers on the coach bench beside him. "A pity you're not wearing your spectacles. I brought it with me."

"I would love to take it home with me and share my thoughts on it with you later."

Instead of being disappointed that the omission of her spectacles had deprived him of her immediate opinion on his new piece, he was rather happy that he was extending his meetings with her. As long as she was with him she could not be with one of her unworthy suitors.

"Have you followed through on my suggestion about having your essays bound in a nice volume?" she asked.

"I have made an appointment to speak with the printer here in Bath tomorrow morning."

"I know the cost must be very dear."

He nodded. "A London printer had given me some idea of how much money it would take, and it will take all the money I can get my hands on."

Her face fell.

"I wouldn't undertake the printing if I were not going to present copies to my family and friends, and that certainly includes you, Miss Arbuckle."

"Money could not purchase anything that I would rather have. I do thank you for considering me."

As they rode on, it suddenly occurred to him that the rose scent was hers. Was this, too, part of Glee's fancying up?

"So, tell me, what will your rebuttal say?" she asked.

He shrugged. "Were you writing a rebuttal, what would you say?"

As she always did, she pondered his question for a few moments in order to articulate a thoughtful response. "I should either make up a scenario that demonstrates the benefits of paying higher wages, or I would do my best to try to find an actual example of such a thing in practice." Her brows elevated. "Though I daresay you are not likely to find such an example in England."

"There you are wrong."

Her eyes widened. "I am unaware of any wealthy landowner who is so enlightened."

He was uncommonly proud when he answered. "It is my brother, though he does not care for others to know of the many fine and good things he does for those who are less fortunate."

"You two are so vastly different that I would never have suspected. I daresay you are the one who has initiated your brother's enlightenment."

"Though he does read—and agree with—my essays, I believe that it's his marriage that has transformed my brother. I will own, when he was a bachelor, we were always in opposition, but that is no longer the case. Now that he is a family man, it seems our many similarities have emerged—which is to say, now that he's married he is more like our father."

"I remember Glee making the same observation."

It was only natural that while they were speaking of his family, he bring up the troubling situation that was bothering him. After all, he shared everything with Miss Arbuckle.

But he hesitated. He did not want her to

think unkindly of his mother. Even if Mama had been unkind for many years.

"Has Glee ever spoken to you of my mother?"

Again, she waited a moment to answer. "She told me that your mother is a step-mother to your elder brother."

"Did she say anything else about my mother?"

"Only that there was an estrangement between her husband and his step-mother, but she did not tell me the cause of the estrangement."

Gratified that Glee had not maligned his mother, he pondered how much he was willing to tell his friend. "Gregory and his wife have some justification to be estranged from Mama, but both my mother and I are deeply desirous of mending the rift."

"Christmas is the perfect time to do that."

He smiled at the woman whose thoughts always paralleled his own. "It is up to me to make the proposal to Gregory, and I've been a coward."

"What is the worst that can come of your magnanimous proposal?"

He suddenly realized the worst thing that could happen would be for things to stay as they were now. "Then it is well worth bringing up the subject with my brother. Thank you, Miss Arbuckle."

"I am honored that our friendship enables us to speak of personal matters."

Personal matters, indeed. How he wanted to ask her if there was a particular man whom she was honoring with her affection, but he did not want to hear the answer. He wanted to continue on as he and Miss Arbuckle always had.

Throughout much of the day, they rode though Sydney Gardens, then along most of the streets of Bath and never exhausted their conversation. When the coach finally returned to her house, he said, "I have excessively enjoyed being with you today. I should like to send my brother's coach to your house tomorrow to collect you. I thought an afternoon together in the library at Blankenship House would be an agreeable way for us to pass the time."

Her brows lowered. "As much as I should adore spending the afternoon with you, I must decline. I have made other plans."

He hoped to God she was not going to be with that lecher Appleton!

Chapter 4

The first thing she saw after she said good-bye to Mr. Blankenship on her home's doorstep was *another* bouquet on the sideboard in the entry hall. Glee must be spending a fortune on flowers. All in a vain effort to make Mr. Blankenship jealous.

Her aged parent met her in the corridor. "You've just missed a Mr. Appleton, who brought those violets for you. How popular you've become since you've acquired Lady Sedgewick's castoffs. It's fortunate for my daughter that breeding twins put the extra weight upon the countess."

Her mother was incapable of suppressing an inflection of pride in her voice when she mentioned Lady Sedgewick—friend to her daughter. (And to Miss Arbuckle's mortification, Mama was guilty of boring her own friends by casually working into every conversation, "My Mary's friends, Lady Sedgewick and the Earl of Sedgewick's two sisters. They were together at Miss Worth's School for Young Ladies, you know.")

"I am not sorry to have missed Mr. Appleton. By comparison to my dear Mr.

Blankenship, his company would have been tiresome."

Her mother's eyes narrowed. "May I remind you that Mr. Blankenship treats you only as a *friend*. Other men may wish to offer you something more."

Even though her mother spoke only out of love, her words wounded Miss Arbuckle. She had never before realized how disappointed her mother was in her failure to attract a husband.

Mary nodded, then spun away. She could not allow her mother to see that she was on the verge of erupting into tears. She clutched Mr. Blankenship's partial essay more tightly in her hands and began to mount the creaking wooden stairs. "I am most anxious to read this piece that Mr. Blankenship has asked my opinion of."

In her bedchamber, she sat near the fire. Before she began to read Mr. Blankenship's work, she wished to recall the many things she and he had so freely discussed that day. She had not enjoyed herself so much since he had left Bath at the end of the summer.

More than anything, she glowed. Never before had he consulted her regarding a personal matter. How honored she was! And more than once today he had told her she was his dearest friend. Clearly, in so many vital ways, he regarded her as she regarded him.

Was there any hope that his deep friendship could turn into something even deeper?

Her thoughts flitted to Melvin and Catherine Steffington. The day she had heard that they were marrying was unquestionably the most shocking day in Miss Mary Arbuckle's life. She would have wagered the roof over their head that the serious twin was incapable of even noticing if a woman happened to be lovely.

If Melvin Steffington could fall in love, then so could Jonathan Blankenship!

She wondered if she had done the right thing by putting all her trust in Glee. Glee had been the one to tell her that under no circumstances was she to consent to see Jonathan Blankenship two days in a row. "Make him believe you have other callers," Glee had insisted.

Oh, how Miss Arbuckle wished she would have been permitted to see him again on the morrow!

She took the crumpled pages of his essay and went searching her bedchamber for her spectacles.

* * *

Though he would rather contemplate his special friendship with Miss Arbuckle, Jonathan knew he must act upon his

Christmas scheme no later than today.

Gregory was not at home when Jonathan returned. Which was just as well. For Jonathan had decided he would first speak to Glee.

As he climbed the stairs to her private study, his heart hammered. At the opened doorway of her green and gilt chamber he stood for a few seconds, watching her scribbling away at her French desk. "I beg a private word with you."

Her face brightened. "Pray, close the door."

He eased the door shut, then came to sit upon the silken settee.

With more than her customary exuberance, Glee did not wait for him to speak. "Are you going to tell me you've come to your senses and realized Miss Arbuckle is the perfect mate for you?"

Her unexpected comment stunned him. Whatever he had planned to say vanished from his mind like paper tossed upon fire. "Good lord, no! Miss Arbuckle and I are friends. Nothing more. I don't know what could possibly have given you such a ridiculous notion!" But he did have some idea. He and Glee both knew that Miss Arbuckle was seeking a husband. More's the pity, he thought with a deep sense of loss.

"Oh." She sounded decidedly disappointed. "Then what did you wish to discuss?"

He quickly repressed any notion of being wed to Miss Arbuckle. "My mother."

She stiffened in much the same way Gregory did when his step-mother was mentioned. "Oh."

"Surely you've noticed that she is eager to be grandmama to Gregory's and your children."

Glee nodded. "She has been very kind in that regard."

"I will be honest with you," Jonathan said. "I thought this Christmas would be a good time to reunite this family. I know there has been disharmony, and my mother is far from being blameless, but I know too that she has come to regret her past mistreatment of Gregory."

Her eyes unusually cold, Glee asked, "She has told you this?"

He nodded. "I thought the time had come to pull up the carpets and sweep out all the bad things that had lain beneath them for too long."

"So you confronted her over her mistreatment of my husband when he was young? Mind you, I did *not* learn of this from Blanks, who refuses to discuss it."

Now Glee again reminded him of an a cub's angry mother. "I did, and she most sincerely grieves because of her former behavior. She wants to atone."

Anxiety gripped his gut as he awaited her response. Though normally impetuous, Glee was taking her sweet time forming an answer to the request that had been so bloody difficult for him to make. He thought of Miss Arbuckle's comment upon his dread. He had nothing to lose and a great deal to gain.

Finally Glee favored him with a smile. "There is no better time than Christmas for a conciliation between Blanks and Aurora. It would make for the truest validation of the Christmas spirit. "

"I had hoped you and Blanks would see it that way."

"Please understand I don't speak for Blanks. What I propose is that we not tell him she is coming. I believe my husband is possessed of a generous enough nature that he will see her presence as a peace offering and will then welcome her."

She was probably right. Gregory was one of the kindest-hearted persons Jonathan had ever known. Still, not consulting his brother troubled Jonathan. Was there a possibility Gregory would be cold to Mama? Jonathan would feel wretched if that happened since the family's Christmas reunification was all his idea. "I would feel better if Gregory had the opportunity to approve the plan."

"It will be better this way. Just think, Jonathan, how heartwarming it will be to see each of them affirm a new beginning. Just like Christmas celebrates a new birth."

"Are you sure?"

"I will not lie. I don't know how Blanks will react to Aurora's visit. Clearly, she's changing, and I believe he will be touched that she has made that first step toward a truce."

"She has truly become a changed person."

"Oh, Jonathan, it will be the best Christmas ever. I felt it as soon as I learned you desired to spend it with us. Now it will be even better. I'm also bursting with the good news that my brother is coming for Christmas. It will be the first time all three of us siblings have been together on December 25 since before the three of us were married."

His brows lowered. "Your house will be far too crowded---Mama and I- - -"

She held up her palm. "My brother and Sally are not going to be staying here, Silly! You forget Thomas Moreland owns the largest home within in thirty miles of Bath. We'll all be gathering there at Winston Hall on Christmas Day."

He hoped to God that if Gregory meant to turn a blind eye to Mama's overture, he would bloody well do so before all their families gathered at Winston Hall.

For some unaccountable reason, as Glee reached for her correspondence, his thoughts turned to her initial statement about him coming to realize that Miss Arbuckle would make him a perfect wife. Of course she would, but nothing could be in greater opposition to his desires.

Jonathan did not want a wife. True, if he were the marrying kind—which he most certainly was not—no one could be more perfect for him than the dear lady.

Just thinking of her wedded to an undeserving rake like Appleton, though, made Jonathan feel as if he could wield a sword in defense of her honor.

He had a very good mind to locate the reprobate and warn him off.

The door to Glee's study eased open, and his brother entered the chamber. Gregory nodded to Jonathan, then moved to his wife and tenderly planted a soft kiss at her neck. "How is my love?"

She whirled around, circled her arms about her still-bent-over husband, and kissed him. "I am excessively happy, if you must know."

He straightened up. "Why is that, dearest?"

"George and Sally are coming to Winston Hall for Christmas!"

"Your brother's leaving Hornsby Manor? I say, that is not in the least indicative of the old stick he's become."

"Fortuitously, he has the devil of a time

refusing Felicity any request. She begged that he come to us for Christmas."

Gregory's brows lowered. "Will they bring the twins?"

"You have to ask? You know what besotted parents those two are."

"Are the babes not awfully young for such a journey?"

"Oh, fi! The motion of the coach will have the little darlings sleeping the entire time."

"I suppose you're right. Speaking of little darlings, where is my son?"

"*Our* son is sleeping, but I believe Joy has heard her Papa's voice."

Her little footsteps sounded in the corridor, then she stood at the opened door. "Papa's home!" She raced to launch herself into his arms, then once in her father's embrace, she eyed her uncle and squirmed away. "Uncle Jona-fin!"

Jonathan melted anew each time he heard himself addressed as the perfect little creature's uncle. He reached down and scooped her into his arms, unconsciously pressing kisses into her mass of golden ringlets. Despite that she was not possessed of red hair, this child was every bit her mother's image.

"Will you give me a piggy-back ride?"

"Only very good little girls get piggy-back rides. Have you been very good?" Jonathan asked.

Her eyes rounded ever so slightly as her anxious gaze moved to her mother, then to her father for confirmation, a confirmation they teasingly withheld.

Then tender-hearted Gregory could stand it no longer. "I think Joy's been a good little girl, don't you, Mama?"

"Today, yes. Not once did she try to steal away her brother's little satin pillow."

Jonathan hoisted Joy onto his shoulders and began moving in a serpentine fashion from room to room until he returned to Glee's study—and Joy's awaiting nurse.

"Come now, Miss Joy," the nurse urged, and the little girl reluctantly left.

"Will you not come in the library with me, Jonathan?" Gregory asked. "We've hardly had a chance to speak to one another since you arrived."

"I was already on my way there."

The library was a comforting chamber of small proportions, but no expense had been spared in fitting the room with hand-carved mahogany shelving from floor to ceiling on all four walls. The shelves displayed fine leather-bound books, many of them rare editions. Jonathan swelled with pride as he recalled that his and Gregory's generation was now the fourth generation to value books and the collecting of them so highly.

Directly opposite the entry a marble fireplace centered the wall, and above it hung a Gainsborough of Gregory's mother, who died giving him life. It was a portrait Jonathan's mother had banished to the attics before Gregory came of age and placed it in a position of prominence in his own house.

Jonathan had to own that his father's first wife was possessed of stunning beauty, and though she was utterly feminine, the resemblance between her and her son was strong.

They settled down on the sumptuous crimson velvet sofa from which they could view the fire blazing in the hearth. "I cannot tell you how happy I am there are no assemblies or musicales tonight," Gregory said. "On a cold night like this, it's good to stay put in one's warm home."

For the first time ever, Jonathan understood his brother's contentment. Family was vital to one's happiness, and Gregory had a wife upon whom he doted and the two most precious children in all the kingdom. And no doubt about it, his family loved Gregory most devotedly.

There had been many instances in Jonathan's life when he had been jealous of his elder brother. It had always seemed to him that Gregory received in abundance all the things a man could desire. Not just the wealth that came from being the first son, but the tall, athletic body and excessive handsomeness; the congeniality that made him popular; facility with every endeavor from sport to mathematics. Even Jonathan's one single crowning achievement—excellence at scholarship—had been matched by his gifted older brother.

Yet, as Jonathan had matured and settled comfortably, he ceased to be jealous of Gregory. He had come to view his own life with the same acceptance as does a husband who falls madly in love with the plain woman he was forced to wed.

But as evening fell across the frigid city on this December night, Jonathan found himself oddly envious of his brother. No one could ever have recommended marriage more effectively than Gregory with his beautiful family and a home filled with love and warmth.

"Indeed," Jonathan said. "It is very good to know one does not have to get out tonight."

"Can I get you Madera?"

Jonathan nodded, then watched as his brother poured.

"I wish to ask you a question," Jonathan said.

Gregory smiled sheepishly as he handed him the glass. "Do not tell me you've finally come to your senses about Miss Arbuckle."

Why in the bloody hell did people think he wished to marry Miss Arbuckle? He glared at his brother. "Surely you, of all people, should know me well enough to know of my firm resolve to stay a bachelor."

"You forget, dear brother, I too was once possessed of such resolve."

Politeness decreed that he not remind Gregory of his significant financial incentive to marry—an incentive that Jonathan would never have.

"I am hardly in a position to take on a wife."

"I have always thought you understood that once you settle on a wife I could buy you a house in Bath. One can live rather cheaply here, and I know you are cautious with your expenditures."

Jonathan's eyes widened. "I understood no such thing, but it matters not. I have no intentions of marrying."

Gregory sighed. "Glee will be most disappointed."

"I am strongly possessed of the notion that your wife is behind Miss Arbuckle's metamorphosis." He studied his brother for a reaction, but there was none. "It is just like Glee to go putting notions of being married into Miss Arbuckle's superior head. I don't know what I should do if she were to marry. You know she's—even more so now that

Melvin Steffington has wed—my dearest friend."

"You ought to marry her, then. A man could do worse. How many men can say their wife is their best friend? Besides me, of course. I cannot too highly praise the magic of sharing every day of your life with the one person most calculated to give you pleasure."

When one put it like that, marriage did not sound so bloody distasteful.

"What I wanted to ask you," Jonathan continued, "Is, if I want to find Appleton tomorrow, where would I go?"

"I'd suggest you try his house on Camden Crescent first. Failing to find him there, you might try Mrs. Vale's."

Jonathan's brows hiked up. Good lord, Mrs. Vale was a well-known courtesan! How could the reprobate even think of calling upon one of unblemished virtue like Miss Arbuckle while conducting an alliance with a tart? It simply was not to be tolerated.

In fact, Jonathan would call him out, but Appleton, being enamored of fisticuffs and activities that involved considerable strength and movement, would likely deprive Jonathan of life in a matter of minutes.

And then dear Miss Arbuckle would be deprived of her protector. Inept as he was.

* * *

Later than night, after the house had gone

dark and quiet, he lay in his bed, thinking of his plans for the next day. He must not forget to go to the printers. It was imperative that he get his writings bound into attractive books to present as Christmas gifts to his family members. And Miss Arbuckle. Even if it would take every last cent he possessed.

Then his thoughts veered off into unfamiliar territory. He bolted up in bed as it suddenly occurred to him he had *another* selection to be bound. This once, in a true gesture of friendship to his dearest friend, he knew it would make him far happier to make her Christmas brighter than to gratify his own vanity. After all, the poor lady had neither father nor brother. And though he and she had never before exchanged Christmas gifts, he knew it was time to start.

He had never been more certain that she was his best friend.

He left the bed and gathered up the pages he would take to the printers in the morning, then returned to bed, disappointed that he would not be able to see her until he went to the Assembly Rooms the following night.

Once more, his thoughts returned to the silly notion Glee and Gregory both had that he should marry Miss Arbuckle, then he thought of his brother's perfect marriage. He was well aware that his brother and Glee shared a bed in the room next to his, and once again he grew strangely envious of them.

Despite that he was visiting in a home where he was loved, he had never felt lonelier. The lonesome howl of December winds seemed to be mocking him. He hoped it was not a portent of when Mama arrived. For he had hurriedly sent off his letter to her in the evening post, urging her to join them by Christmas Day.

He thought of Miss Arbuckle, and the scent of roses became so vivid he almost thought she was here in his bedchamber. His pulse accelerated. He wondered anew what other plans were depriving him of her company tomorrow. *By, God, if it's Appleton, I'll wring his lecherous neck.*

She was very dear to him, but not in a romantic way. Until Glee mentioned today the possibility of him marrying Miss Arbuckle, such a thought had never once crossed his mind. He had never before realized a sensible woman like she would fancy being wed. Just as he had never before fancied the idea of being wed.

He had always been exceptionally content to be alone. He had his writing. And his books. And friendship with the likes of Miss Arbuckle.

He had never minded being in a cold, lonely bed.

Until tonight.

Chapter 5

The following morning as Jonathan was filling his tea cup from the spigot of the silver urn, the butler came to the door of the morning room and addressed Gregory. "Sir, there's an exceedingly ill kept woman at your back door begging a word with you or the missus. I tried to give her a bite to eat with the intention of sending her upon her way, but she refused sustenance and insisted you knew her."

Glee's rounded eyes met her husband's. "Do you think it could be Mrs. A?"

Gregory whirled around, brows lowered. "Is she a young woman who's terribly thin?"

"Indeed, you have just described her," the butler said.

Gregory and Glee both leapt from their chairs. "Do show her in. Is her lad with her?"

"I saw no boy. Are you sure you want her in your home? She looks as if she sorely needs a bath."

"Yes, please, Hampton," Glee answered.

Jonathan cleared his throat. "Should you like me to leave the chamber?"

"We have nothing to hide from you," Glee

said. "You may have heard us discussing the woman at Mr. Willowby's building. . ."

"Oh, yes. The. . ." Jonathan lowered his voice. "The soaker?"

Gregory nodded grimly.

Jonathan trained his attention upon the buttering of his toast, but when the woman came to the doorway, he was powerless not to take a look at the emaciated young woman dressed in many layers of ragged, dirty clothing.

"Thank ye, Mr. Blankenship, for allowing me to come in yer fine home. I know it's been a great long while since ye kindly offered to bring me and me lad into yer service, and I know how poorly I must look, but I was wondering if the offer is still available."

"Of course it is," Glee said.

Gregory held up a stern hand to his wife. "With conditions."

"I'm willing to do whatever it takes. Me lad ain't never 'ad a proper Christmas, and I've decided I've been far too selfish for far too long."

"Then you're willing to give up your gin?" Gregory asked.

She nodded, not without a pained expression on her thin face. "If I don't, me boy will be an orphan by next Christmas."

"And you're willing to live under our roof by our rules?"

"I should be honored to live under this fine roof."

"We will provide everything you need," Gregory said. "New clothing for you. You shouldn't need to bring anything when you come—other than Archie."

"And any items of sentimentality you might be attached to," Glee added.

Even from where Jonathan sat, he caught a whiff of a stale gin.

"I've got nothin' save me precious son."

"You realize that since Archie's so good with horses, he will be a groom and will sleep in a room above the stables?" Gregory asked.

She nodded. "He's been beggin me for a long while. He ain't never 'ad a proper home. He wanted us to 'ave the security of home that didn't change on a whim. And ye know how he loves 'orses."

"He's very good with them," Gregory said.

She favored them with a shy smile. "Then I can go tell Archie?"

"First," Gregory cautioned, "you must agree to our conditions. Though you will have your own chamber with a comfortable bed and fire every night, you must know that until you are accustomed to your new life, you will be locked in your chamber each night. Your chamber will be unlocked at dawn, when your day's work begins."

She nodded gravely.

"And you will have to allow our housekeeper, Mrs. Roberts, to help bathe you and supply you with fresh new clothing."

"She ain't gonna want me 'ere."

"Do not judge her until you know her," Glee said.

Gregory held the young woman in his somber gaze. "Remember always, a good servant does what her master says. And we expect Mrs. Roberts to be a good servant."

"Provided," Glee added, "that the master does not demand the servant do something that is immoral or illegal."

"And I give you my word," Gregory said, addressing the woman with the greatest kindness, "we will never ask you to do either one of those things."

"I know yer a good man."

"It's so beastly cold," Glee said, "allow us to take you to fetch Archie in our coach. If you could just give us a minute to finish breakfast."

"Please, help yourself to any food you'd like," Gregory added.

Mrs. A. shook her head. "I ain't got no appetite, but I should be 'appy to take me boy a bit of toast."

Glee rang for a servant, and when Hampton returned asked that cook prepare a breakfast for them to take to a hardy lad.

Jonathan hurried with his own breakfast.

"If it's agreeable to you, I'd like to catch a ride in your coach. I need to visit the printers this morning."

"Certainly," his brother answered.

* * *

When the coach reached the building where his brother's solicitor kept chambers, Jonathan stayed in the coach and watched as the other three disembarked and approached the excited lad. The boy, who looked to be around ten, looked far more well fed than his mother. Then Jonathan recalled that some time back, Glee had made arrangements to supply one meal a day for the lad—and his mother, if only she'd eat.

"Can I watch yer 'orses, Mr. Blankenship?"

Gregory ruffled the lad's hair. "Indeed you can. In fact, you're going to start caring for all my horses every day."

Archie suspiciously eyed his mother, who nodded, smiling. "It's true, me lad. We're going into service for the Blankenships. It's me first Christmas gift to me fine son."

Archie buried his face into his mother's skirts. Jonathan realized the boy did not want the others to see him crying.

Crying tears of joy.

From there, they went to the printer's. "Whatever are you having printed?" Glee asked him.

"I had intended to have my essays bound

into books for Christmas presents to my family, but my plans were destroyed by an uncharacteristic burst of altruism to a dear friend."

Glee's eyes rounded, then her gaze dropped to the papers he clutched in his hands. "May I see?"

He handed them to her.

A brilliant smiled alighted her face when she scanned the pages.

* * *

The coach waited while he was inside the printer's. On the return to Queen Square, Glee said, "I've asked the coachman to just drive by Guinea Lane. I don't intend to call on the Arbuckles. I merely wanted to see if Appleton might be visiting Miss Arbuckle today."

Jonathan's brows lowered. "How would you be able to tell if it's his vehicle?"

"Oh, since you were last in Bath, he's gotten a very fine new coach," Glee said. "It has the family coat of arms upon the door."

As their coach approached Guinea Lane, Jonathan's stomach once again began doing that thing it did upon eating rotten food. It would make him excessively angry were he to learn that lout was calling upon Miss Arbuckle.

When they turned onto Guinea Lane, he became truly sick when he saw the shiny new coach in front of Miss Arbuckle's. He glared at Glee. "Are you happy with yourself now? You know the man is unfit for someone as pure as Miss Arbuckle."

"I beg that you not malign my friends," Gregory said.

"I'll say nothing behind his back I wouldn't say to his face," Jonathan countered.

"Then you can tell him yourself at the Assembly Rooms tonight."

"I just very well may!" Yesterday, he would have had no courage against a sport-mad fellow like Appleton. What in the devil had come over him in a single day's time?

* * *

Jonathan was gratified that his sister-in-law had arranged to once again pick up Miss Arbuckle for the assembly, owing to the cold. He wouldn't put it past that Appleton to try to get a fetching-looking thing like Miss Arbuckle in his shiny new carriage for lascivious purposes.

Once the heavily bundled lady was seated beside him in the coach, Glee addressed her. "Did I tell you my brother and Sally are coming to Winston Hall for Christmas?"

"How wonderful!" Miss Arbuckle could not suppress the joy from her sweet voice. "This will be their first Christmas in Bath since they married, is it not?"

"Yes, it will be a very merry gathering.

Felicity has asked me to invite you and your mother to share the Christmas goose with us. Thomas plans to send his coach for you, if that is agreeable to you."

"It is very kind of you to remember us," Miss Arbuckle said. "I suppose your family *is* the closest thing we have to family."

"All of us—me, Felicity, and Sally—do think of you almost as a sister."

Oddly, Jonathan rather warmed to the idea of having Miss Arbuckle be part of his family.

When they reached the Assembly Rooms, he assisted her in removing her outer garments and was once again displeased that so much of her delicate skin was exposed. His gaze whisked over her bare flesh to the graceful drape of the soft yellow gown she wore.

She looked up at him, smiling.

"Will you do me the goodness of standing up with me the first set?" he asked, most determinedly preventing his greedy gaze from dropping to her plump breasts. What the devil had come over him? In the past four years he'd never precisely thought of her as a woman, and now he could not purge his mind of her femininity.

On the dance floor, they faced each other on the longway, and again, he eyed the bodice of her pretty saffron-coloured gown, but the true attraction was what filled the bodice.

Unlike other men, he'd never been terribly aware of those . . . things, but now he imagined what it would be like to . . . Dear God! What was he thinking! This was dear Miss Arbuckle, not some doxy!

When it was their turn to clutch hands and gracefully move down the longway together, he could have burst with pride that this lovely creature was *his*.

His great friend, that is. Though as he thought on it, he liked to think of Miss Arbuckle as *his*. Somewhat in the same way Gregory fancied Glee.

Which meant. . . Good lord! He lost count of his steps and stumbled. His pulse rocketed.

Instead of being embarrassed over her partner's incompetence, she favored him with a sweet smile, and he was swamped with a sense of well-being.

It was while they were dancing that he saw Appleton, standing in the doorway with Sir Elvin and eying Miss Arbuckle with an arrogant smirk.

The time had come for Jonathan to assert himself as her protector.

When the dance was finished, he walked Miss Arbuckle to the scarlet settee next to Glee, then strode up to Appleton and Sir Elvin, just as Gregory joined them.

"Are you looking for my twin?" Sir Elvin

asked Jonathan.

"No." Jonathan's gaze bore into Appleton's face as if drawn by a magnet. "I have come to demand that you cease showering your attentions upon Miss Arbuckle."

Gregory's mouth dropped open. "Now see here, old boy, you can't go ordering my friends about like that."

"Miss Arbuckle has no brothers, no father," said Jonathan. "It is for me to defend her honor."

Appleton's eyes widened. "Are you saying that you are betrothed to the lady?"

"I am not betrothed to the lady, but I am far more suited for her than you will ever be!"

"I believe I have more to offer the lady than you do," Appleton challenged.

"Miss Arbuckle is not interested in wealth."

Appleton tossed his head back and laughed. "The woman has not been born who is disinterested in wealth." His face hardened, and he came close enough to Jonathan that Jonathan could smell the brandy upon his breath. "If you weren't Blanks's little brother, I'd call you out!"

"Go ahead!" Jonathan shouted. *Dear God, what am I getting myself into?* What happened to his life-long cowardice? Appleton was not only considerably larger than Jonathan, he was also well trained in pugilism, sword fighting, and shooting. *I am a dead man.*

Gregory wedged himself between the two men, shouting, "I will not permit this! Appleton's had too much to drink, and neither of you know what you're doing. Why do you not go declare yourself to Miss Arbuckle, Jonathan?" It had been many years since Gregory had directed such a searing gaze upon Jonathan.

It suddenly became clear to Jonathan what he had to do. He had to do this for himself.

Chapter 6

"You must have confidence in my ability to read human nature," Glee told Miss Arbuckle after Mr. Blankenship left her at Glee's settee. "Jonathan is exceptionally vexed with Appleton." Glee lowered her voice. "I most cleverly arranged that we would drive past your house this morning whilst I knew Appleton would be there."

Miss Arbuckle's eyes rounded. "You asked Mr. Appleton to visit me, did you not?"

"Of course I did. And you must believe me when I tell you that Jonathan could not conceal his anger."

Miss Arbuckle could barely concentrate on Glee's words when she witnessed Mr. Blankenship storming across the ballroom floor and greeting Mr. Appleton. Even though it was Sir Elvin who addressed him, Jonathan Blankenship could not remove his angry gaze from Mr. Appleton.

"You must not watch Jonathan," Glee cautioned. "Do not permit him to see that you're concerned."

"I cannot heed you," Miss Arbuckle snapped with uncharacteristic sharpness.

"Can you not see that poor Jonathan may very well be initiating fisticuffs with Mr. Appleton, who is considerably larger than him! Do you really think I am the cause of this scene?"

"Of course you are! Jonathan's in love with you. Have I not told you that any number of times?"

Miss Arbuckle turned an anguished face upon her friend. "We must do something! I would die if something should happen to Jonathan." Twice now, she had referred to the man she loved by his Christian name.

"Blanks will handle the situation, never fear. See, he's stepped up and is acting commanderly. Is that a word?"

"I don't believe it is."

"Being a talented poet, you would know."

Miss Arbuckle whirled at Glee. "How can you discuss something so frivolous at a time like this? What if it were your dear Blanks who was being threatened?"

"Trust Blanks to handle the fracas."

Once Miss Arbuckle saw that the elder Blankenship brother had indeed stepped between the two near-combatants, her tightly fisted hands began to uncoil.

Then Jonathan stormed away. When he began to walk toward her, she forced herself to look away. Glee said she must not look too eager for his attentions. Even though she was. She would never understand the coy rituals young ladies engaged in. Why could she not just allow herself to be honest? Because pretty ladies did not risk scorn by admitting their attraction to a man; plain and penniless old maids could admit no such thing.

When he was within ten feet of her, she slowly turned to him. Their eyes met and held as he closed the gap that separated them. "Will you permit me to walk in the Octagon with you?" he asked in a voice that did not seem like Jonathan Blankenship's.

"Yes, of course." She tried to act calm as she placed her hand upon his proffered arm, but she was trembling. There was about him a demeanor she had never before seen. An intensity that frightened her. She prayed he was not going to tell her that he and Mr. Appleton were meeting at dawn.

The very thought had her stomach roiling. She could not ignore the anger she had seen on Jonathan's beloved face when he spoke to Mr. Appleton. Could Glee be right about the source of his anger? Could Mary Arbuckle possibly be the cause of that fury? Even if it would make her appear conceited, she felt compelled to address the matter. "Pray, Mr. Blankenship, are you out of charity with Mr. Appleton?"

"I hate to even hear that vile man's name

upon your lips." They had reached the Octagon, but few others shared it with them since it was so early in the evening's proceedings. It was much quieter here. He stopped. Candlelight from a wall sconce just above his head cast light on his mahogany hair. It struck her that the dark hair was the only physical trait he and his brother shared. Jonathan was less tall, and to others he might appear less handsome. But not to her. She could never tire of Jonathan's patrician face that bespoke his intelligent mind.

He took both her hands in his. "I must beg that you not see that man. He is unfit for you."

She knew Glee would scorn her, but Mary Arbuckle could no longer portray herself as something she wasn't. Her heart fluttering madly because Jonathan was holding her hands, she spoke. "You are right. We would never suit, Mr. Appleton and me."

His green eyes widened. "Is there another man with whom you would suit?"

She drew in a deep breath and prepared herself for possible humiliation, for the possibility that what she was about to declare could effectively terminate their friendship.

It was a risk she must take.

"There has ever been only one man to whom I am suited. Surely you know that."

A stab of fear flinched across his angular

face. "I hope you're speaking of me." His hands tightened.

"Only you. Please do not deny what we both know."

His mouth softened into a smile. "I've denied it for too long when it should have been as apparent as the nose upon my face. I have always been happiest when I am with you."

His simmering gaze heated her very blood.

She swallowed hard. "Me, too."

"I've been wretched all week, worrying you would marry a man not worthy of you. Then it finally occurred to me that I could be your husband. Oh, my dear Mary, I'm begging for your hand in marriage."

Her eyes watered, and she vigorously nodded. "That is what I've always wanted." It occurred to her that she was indebted to Glee for this moment. Would it ever have come without Glee's scheme?

"I've a deuced strong desire to kiss you," he said huskily.

She nodded. How she would love to feel his lips upon hers!

"But as this is a most public place, I would never do anything that would sully your good name." He sighed. "I just had a stupendous thought."

"What, my love?"

Love shone in his eyes when he looked at

her. "Your name will soon be Blankenship. You've made me very happy."

"Me, too."

"I feel as if I'm an uncaged bird. I don't want to go back into the ballroom. We have much to discuss, plans to be made, my dearest Mary." He leaned toward her until their foreheads bumped. "I will claim my beloved for the last waltz."

"I should like to feel myself in your arms."

"Oh, God, Mary."

* * *

In the coach ride home from the Assembly Rooms, Jonathan and Mary held hands. "I know this will come as no surprise to you two," Jonathan said to Gregory and Glee, "But Mary has made me the happiest man in the kingdom by consenting to become my wife."

Glee began to squeal. "I am ever so happy! I knew you two loved each other!"

"I think everyone knew it except Jonathan," Gregory said.

"I declare, I never saw two people so well suited. When will you marry?"

Jonathan pressed his lips to Mary's gloved hand. "As soon as my brother purchases us a house." He turned to his betrothed. "Your mother may reside with us, if she would like, love."

It seemed incredible what a difference one

day made. He had never felt lonelier than he had the previous night; now, he was bursting with happiness, now that he would have his very own family. He was anxious to introduce Mary to Mama. Mama would have to love her.

"We shall start looking tomorrow," Gregory said. "Even if it is Christmas Eve."

"I shall need the coach. I mean to look for presents for . . . Archie and his mother . . . and perhaps someone else," Glee said.

Jonathan knew Glee wanted to get something for his mother.

"You leave Archie's present to me," Gregory said. "I have something in mind."

When the coach pulled up in front of the Arbuckle's house, Jonathan disembarked, then turned back to help Mary down. Arm in arm, they strolled to the door.

"I don't want this night to be over with," she said. "I don't want to part from you."

"Soon, love, we'll be together. Forever."

They both climbed the pair of steps, then faced each other. He drew her into his arms and lowered his lips to capture hers for a breathless, incredibly satisfying kiss. Nothing had ever stirred him so profoundly.

When he finished thoroughly kissing the woman who owned his heart, he said, "When we marry, I should like for you to wear that yellow dress. But only for me. I shouldn't like any other man gawking at your . . . well, surely you know of what jiggly bits I refer to."

"Only you," she murmured.

* * *

When they entered the home on Queen Square, the drawing room was ablaze with bright lights. "What the devil?" Gregory said, striding to the chamber.

And there stood his step-mother.

Jonathan watched as Gregory froze. "I expect you could not bear to not share Christmas with your son."

"With both my sons," she said somberly. "Please, Gregory, forgive me. I know it's no excuse, but my mistreatment of you—which I can finally own up to—was because I was so insanely jealous of your mother. Your father may have remarried quickly after her death, but his heart always belonged to your mother. And because you looked like her, I took it out upon you." She stepped toward Gregory. "Can you ever forgive me?"

Overcome with powerful emotions, Gregory merely nodded. He crossed the room and drew her into his arms. "Thank you for coming. This is the happiest Christmas of my life."

Later, Jonathan moved to his mother and embraced her. "This is undoubtedly the best Christmas I've ever had. It is my pleasure to tell you, Mama, that I have become betrothed."

She squeezed him most affectionately. "I do hope you've asked Miss Arbuckle to be your wife."

"How did you know about Miss Arbuckle?"

"I have known for a very long time that you were in love with her. Pray, son, what did it take to force you to make a declaration?" She gave him a cocky smile.

His gaze flicked to Glee. "I believe I owe Glee a very great debt of gratitude."

Chapter 7

Jonathan was out of charity with his brother. "I don't see why I have to apologize to Appleton. I'm still angry that he was engaging in a flirtation with my future wife at the same time as he was cavorting with the likes of Mrs. Vale!"

"Glee will want to murder me for telling you this, but I think my wife asked Appleton to pay special attention to Miss Arbuckle in order to awaken your own desire for the lady."

"That was a wicked thing to do!"

"Are you not excessively happy today?"

"I am. I've never been happier." The only thing that could make him happier was to have his dear Mary beside him right now.

"Then you are indebted to my wife and her scheming—though I will own Appleton did admit that he found Miss Arbuckle *bang up to scratch.*"

The coach pulled up to Appleton House. *I must repress any desire to slam a fist into that man's face*, Jonathan told himself as he climbed from the coach.

They were soon face-to-face with Appleton,

who was holding a small dog. He stiffened when he saw Jonathan.

"I have come to offer my apologies," Jonathan said, "for my unpardonable behavior. I could not tolerate that another man was paying addresses to the woman I plan to wed."

Appleton's thin face brightened. "I say, old thing, felicitations and all that to you both. She's a fine lady."

That wasn't so bad. "Thank you."

"Now, we shall take that pup off your hands," Gregory said.

Appleton affectionately ruffled the fur on the dog's neck. "I know the lad will be happy with it."

Jonathan's brows hiked. "Is not little Gregory too small for a pup?"

"Oh, this isn't for my son. It's for young Archie." It was impossible for Gregory to prevent a note of pride from slipping into his voice whenever he said *my son*.

"Ah, the urchin's Christmas present!" Jonathan said. "What lad wouldn't love a furry little beast to call his own?"

Gregory nodded. "Especially a lad who's never had anything—not even a home. At present, Glee's having a small bed moved into the mother's chamber so their little family can be together at Christmas. Like ours."

"Yes. Like ours."

* * *

She knew she was going to see Jonathan on Christmas Day. He had promised to call on her so they could go together to the morning church service, and she had already planned what she would wear. She would wear one of her old dresses. To please him.

But how would she make it through this Christmas Eve without seeing him? No day had ever seemed longer. It was nearly four in the afternoon—and nearly dark, which was customary this time of the year.

As she sat by the lamp table in the drawing room rereading his unfinished essay for the tenth time, there was a knock upon the front door. Since their two servants were free of duties on Christmas Eve and Christmas Day, she went to answer the knock herself. It could not be Jonathan because she had heard no carriage wheels in the street.

There stood Jonathan. Even though he was dressed warmly in a great coat and muffler and thick leather gloves, he looked as if he were freezing. His cheeks and nose were so red with cold, she feared he would suffer frost bite. Her eyes widened with concern. "You walked?"

"Are you not going to invite me in?"

"Oh, my dearest! You'll take your death of cold. Please, come in."

After closing the door to the harsh winter

elements, he divested himself of his outer garments. Then she noticed he set down a bag. "Come, love, and stand by the fire," she said.

They went to the drawing room, strode to the fireplace, and faced each other, his heated gaze lazily moving to her *jiggly bits*, which *were* more prominent in this dress, another she had received from Sally Sedgewick.

"I have a desire to take you in my arms and kiss a path to those lovely shoulders." His eyes held hers with intensity.

"The door is closed."

He then did exactly what he'd spoken of, and she thought she had never enjoyed anything so much. Thank God for Sally's dresses! They had certainly brought out the man in him.

And the woman in her.

When he finished, he took her hand. "I have what I hope may be good news."

Her brows arched.

"I've a special license, and the vicar has promised to marry us the day after Christmas. Our wedding trip shall be to Sutton Manor—which we will have all to ourselves."

"That is wonderful news!"

"If you do not mind, my mother—who has come from Sutton Manor—has offered to take our list of desires and find us a house here in Bath whilst we honeymoon."

"I have only one desire, and I think you must know what that is."

"Oh, god, Mary, how am I to stand waiting for two more days?" His gaze went from her to the hearth where he had placed the bag. "I must think of something else, or I'll go mad with want."

He reached down and lifted the bag.

"What is that?" she asked.

"It's your Christmas present."

Her face collapsed. "But I have nothing for you."

"How can you say that? You've given me the most precious of all gifts. And when you see your present, you'll know how much your gift is also a present to me."

Her brows lowered. "What can you mean?"

"Let us sit upon the sofa."

They sat very close together, then he reached into the bag and withdrew a slender book bound in soft green leather.

"Oh, you're giving me a printed copy of your essays! How delightful." She took it, eagerly opened up to the title page, and she went deadly still as her eye ran along the printing, then teared up. "It's not your writings."

"No, love. As I prepared to go to the printers, I realized how conceited I must appear. Then I knew that out of my love for you—which I was still not fully aware of—I must have *your* poems bound. I should like to share you and your incredible talent with the world. I've sent a copy to a London publisher, and I had enough copies made to present them to members of our respective families as Christmas gifts."

She did not want to bawl in front of him, but she could not help it. No one had ever done anything for her in her entire life. Only Mama had ever given her a Christmas gift. Nothing could have affected her more profoundly. There in black and white read *The Golden Bough and Other Poems by Mary Arbuckle.*

She flung her arms around him and wept into his fine woolen coat.

* * *

As he and Mary were leaving the church on Christmas morning, Jonathan glimpsed Archie on the back row. But where was the lad's mother? He hoped to God she hadn't not availed herself of the holiday to get a nip of gin. When they drew abreast of the lad, Jonathan was stunned to realize the woman beside Archie *was* his mother. Layers of grime had been removed from her skin to reveal a complexion nearly as pretty as Mary's ivory skin, with a hint of rose upon the woman's cheeks. Even the woman's hair was clean and tidily arranged. He recalled that Glee had bought her a new cloak for Christmas, and she must be excessively fond of it for she'd worn the blue woolen cape-like thing all through the Christmas service.

What a lovely Christmas this was proving to be!

A short time later he and Mary, along with Mrs. Arbuckle and his own mother, were greeting Thomas and Felicity Moreland and Lord and Lady Sedgewick at Winston Hall. Children were scurrying all about. His precious little niece was thrilled to be with her Moreland cousins. The fact that all three of them were male in no way prevented her from following them about.

Glee had spread out a blanket for the babies to crawl up. Sedgewick's older son and daughter were down on their knees playing with their new twin siblings. The twins—a boy and girl—looked nothing like each other, but each looked remarkably like their elder brother, who was a miniature version of his blond and burly father.

Though Glee had desired that baby Gregory crawl with his cousins, Jonathan's mother was reluctant to have the babe removed from her lap. Jonathan had never known his mother could act so foolish. She kept remarking on how strong was the family resemblance. "I see your dear Papa's face in the little darling," she said. More than once.

Later, whilst they were sitting in the Moreland's opulent dinner room eating the Christmas goose from heavily gilded plates beneath a row of sparkling chandeliers, a heavy knock sounded at the front door. Thomas got to his feet. "I've given most of the servants a Christmas holiday. Allow me to get the door."

A moment later, he returned, a letter in this hand. "A special messenger brought this for Sedgewick."

Lord Sedgewick's brows lowered when Moreland handed it to him.

Why would someone send a special messenger on Christmas Day? What could be so bloody important, Jonathan wondered. All conversation ceased as all eyes went to Sedgewick. When he finished reading, he shook his head in bewilderment as he handed the letter to his wife.

"Pray, what is it?" Felicity asked. "Is everything all right?"

"Indeed it is," a stunned Sedgewick said. "This may very well be my best Christmas ever."

The man already had a wife he loved most potently and four lovely children. What else could a man want, Jonathan wondered.

Sally Sedgewick erupted into tears, burying her face in her hands, her husband drawing her into his chest. "There now, love. Everything will be wonderful from now on."

"You must tell us," Felicity demanded.

George Pembroke, the Earl of Sedgewick, regarded his elder sister. "It's a letter from Mr. Johnson's solicitor with specific instructions that it be delivered to me on Christmas Day."

"Not *that* Mr. Johnson? Evil Becky Johnson's papa?" Felicity asked.

Sedgewick nodded grimly. "It seems that Mr. Johnson intends to leave me his entire fortune to make restitution for the wrongs committed to me by his daughter."

Lady Sedgewick still had not pulled herself together, and her husband was most concerned. "It is all right, love."

"I know. I'm just overcome," she whimpered.

"I heard Mr. Johnson was in Bath to take the waters because he's been very ill," Felicity said.

"And he was awfully old when his only child was born. He must be at least seventy," Glee added.

"Well, I'm going to wish him continued good health," George said.

Lady Sedgewick's calm was soon restored, and the meal resumed.

"My dear brother-in-law has an announcement to make," Glee said, eying

Jonathan, mirth flashing in those vivid green eyes of hers.

Everyone turned to him. He cleared his throat, flashed a smile at Mary, then said, "Miss Arbuckle and I should like to request your presence at the church tomorrow morning. For our wedding." He looked lovingly down at her. "Mary has done me the goodness to consent to be my wife."

Felicity Moreland squealed with delight. "I've been expecting that announcement for years since we all knew you two were perfect for one another."

Lord Sedgewick and Thomas Moreland both left their seats and came to shake Jonathan's hand. "I hope you'll be as happy as Felicity and I," Moreland said.

Lord Sedgewick smiled down upon him as he offered his sturdy handshake. "Felicitations, old boy. I cannot recommend marriage too enthusiastically."

"Now practically every one of our friends will be happily wed," Felicity said.

"There's Appleton," Glee said dryly. "We shall have to find a nice girl for him."

"And for Sir Elvin," Lady Sedgewick added.

"Oh, my goodness! I forgot to tell you," Felicity said. "I got a message last night from Catherine Steffington telling me she was uncommonly happy to announce that yesterday she was delivered of a beautiful baby boy!"

All at once, Felicity was barraged with questions. What did they name the babe? How was Catherine getting along? Was Melvin a proud papa?

Jonathan found himself a bit envious of his old friend Melvin Steffington. Jonathan realized he would enjoy having a son of his own. A son of his and Mary's. He looked up from his plate, feasting his eyes on Mary's sweet profile.

She turned to him, her eyelids shyly downcast.

He lowered his voice to just a whisper, a whisper no one save his beloved could hear. "I should like us to have a child by next Christmas."

Beneath the table, their hands met. He squeezed hers most lovingly, as he watched her pretty brown eyes moistening. "Will I sound bold if I say I should love it above all things to oblige you?"

"Not one of your beautiful poems could sound any lovelier to my ears, dearest."

THE END

The Brides of Bath Series

If you enjoyed reading *A Christmas In Bath*,

you may also enjoy the other five installments of *The Brides of Bath* series*:*

The Bride Wore Blue
(The Brides of Bath, Book 1)

Cheryl Bolen's writing draws you into her fast-paced story. 4 Stars – *Romantic Times*

Cheryl Bolen returns to the Regency England she knows so well. . .If you love a steamy Regency with a fast pace, be sure to pick up The Bride Wore Blue. – *Happily Ever After*

* * *

For six long years Thomas Moreland has dreamed of the beautiful young noblewoman who rescued him from death. While amassing his fortune in India, not a day passed he did not recall Felicity's fair loveliness, did not recall the silken tones of her sweet voice, did not desire to possess her.

Now a widow, Felicity Harrison does not recognize the handsome nabob as the young man left for dead by highwayman years earlier. Though she wants nothing more than to snub the arrogant man who promises to rescue her family from financial ruin in exchange for presenting his sister to Society, she cannot snub him. She must force herself to bear his company. But the longer she is with him, the more she has to force herself to remain true to her dead husband's memory. Why is it the humbly born Thomas Moreland possesses more nobility that any man of her class? And why is it she finds it harder and harder to mourn a dead man when Thomas's virility awakens her deepest desires?

With His Ring
(The Brides of Bath, Book 2)

Texas Gold's Runner-up for Best Historical Romance 2002
Highly recommended. – *Under the Covers*

Cheryl Bolen does it again! There is laughter, and the interaction of the characters pulls you right into the book. I look forward to the next in this series. 4 Stars – *Romantic Times*

With His Ring is a good book. Once you start reading you will not want to put it down. . .The secondary characters are a blast. They will have you laughing right along with Glee's stunts. – *The Romance Readers Connection*

If you liked Cheryl Bolen's first installment in her Brides of Bath series set in Regency England, you'll like this one. With His Ring has plenty of sensuality. – *Happily Ever After*

* * *

Glee Pembroke has turned down countless offers of marriage because she has secretly been in love with her brother's best friend, Gregory Blankenship, all her life. When she learns Gregory will lose his considerable fortune if he's not wed by his twenty-fifth birthday, she persuades him to enter into a sham marriage with her. What he doesn't know is that she plans to win his heart. She will do everything in her power to make him happy—including mimicking the ways of a "fast" woman since he's noted for alliances with women of that sort.

Why did he ever allow himself to marry the maddening Glee? He'd thought they would have great fun, but at every turn, she exasperates him. Why does she persist in wearing the bodice of her dresses so blasted low? Why do other men persist in flirting with her, his wife? And why in the blazes has his heretofore complacent life been turned upside down by this sham marriage? He finds himself longing for a real marriage, but for reasons he cannot divulge, that can never happen.

The Bride's Secret
(The Brides of Bath, Book 3)
*(*Previously titled *A Fallen Woman)*

You'll fall for A Fallen Woman, the latest

Regency romance by Cheryl Bolen. .this emotional story of a woman's journey from despair to triumph has what we all want from a love story. – *In Print*

A story of healing, forgiveness and change that will make readers cheer. – *Romantic Times*

I would recommend A Fallen Woman to anyone." – *Escape to Romance*

* * *

Since his commanding officer in the Peninsula took a bullet meant for him, James Moore, now the Earl of Rutledge, feels responsible for the dead man's young son and the boy's exquisite mother, Carlotta Ennis— so responsible that he offers to marry the lavender-eyed beauty. Though their marriage was not to be a love match, Carlotta's torturing presence has James yearning to make her his true wife.

Though she did not love his lordship, her desperate situation forced her to accept his proposal. Little did she know she would come to crave being with him, would hunger for his every touch. If only she could be worthy of the fine man she's married, if only she can keep him from learning her dark secret . . .

To Take This Lord
(The Brides of Bath, Book 4)
*(*Previously titled *An Improper Proposal)*

"Wonderfully Crafted...
Highly recommended...
 5 stars." – *Huntress Book Reviews*

"Bolen's writing... creates the perfect atmosphere for her enchanting romances." – *Romantic Times*

"Bolen does a wonderful job building simmering sexual tension." – *Booklist*

* * *

Even though it's been two years since his cherished wife died on childbed, George Pembroke, the Viscount Sedgewick, continues to rely on liquor to blunt his grief.

Worried about him and his children, George's sisters urge him to ask spinster Sally Spenser—a longtime family friend—to help care for his daughter and son. Sally's the perfect person. She's of high birth (but has no money) and she adores Lord Sedgewick's children. It's her deep love of the motherless children and fear that their father might marry an unfeeling stepmother that prompt Sally to consider George's proposal. Even though it will be unbearable living under the roof of the man she loves and knowing she can never have him.

Love In The Library
(The Brides of Bath, Book 5)

The Beauty and the Scholar. . .

Certain the "smart" Steffington twin is the person who can help her recover her late husband's nearly priceless stolen Chaucer manuscript, Catherine Bexley tearfully persuades the scholar to assist her. A deal is struck. She's particularly pleased that the Doctor of Letters is not interested in seducing her because she's finished with men (owing to her late husband's multitude of unfortunate alliances with. . .doxies). Regaining the manuscript and its subsequent sale will give her independence to ensure she never has to marry again.

Once he learns the poor, delicate widow is in danger of losing her heavily mortgaged home if they cannot find the valuable hologram, Dr. Melvin Steffington vows to do everything in his power to restore the rare Canterbury Tales to her. It's obvious the pretty little thing needs a man to help her. Not normally the twin to take note of pretty little things, Melvin can't help but to observe that Mrs. Bexley's physical appearance is much like the beauties so admired by his twin brother.

He hadn't counted on the fact he would have to pose as her husband as they race against the banker's ticking clock. He hadn't counted on the mysterious thief attempting to kill him. Most of all, he hadn't counted on how close he would become to the lovely widow or how the kissing of said widow would become the most pleasant experience in his entire seven and twenty years...

Author's Biography

A former journalist and English teacher, Cheryl Bolen sold her first book to Harlequin Historical in 1997. That book, *A Duke Deceived*, was a finalist for the Holt Medallion for Best First Book, and it netted her the title Notable New Author. Since then she has published more than 20 books with Kensington/Zebra, Love Inspired Historical and was Montlake launch author for Kindle Serials. As an independent author, she has broken into the top 5 on the *New York Times* and top 20 on the *USA Today* best-seller lists.

Her 2005 book *One Golden Ring* won the Holt Medallion for Best Historical, and her 2011 gothic historical *My Lord Wicked* was awarded Best Historical in the International Digital Awards, the same year one of her Christmas novellas was chosen as Best Historical Novella by Hearts Through History. Her books have been finalists for other awards, including the Daphne du Maurier, and have been translated into eight languages.

She invites readers to www.CherylBolen.com, or her blog, www.cherylsregencyramblings.wordpress.co or Facebook at https://www.facebook.com/pages/Cheryl-Bolen-Books/146842652076424.